AIRSHIP 27 PRODUCTIONS

Published by Airship 27 Productions
www.airship27.com
www.airship27hangar.com

Interior illustrations © 2014 Richard Serrao
Cover illustration © 2014 Richard Serrao and Shannon Hall

Editor: Ron Fortier
Associate Editor: Jerry Edwards
Marketing and Promotions Manager: Michael Vance
Production and design by Rob Davis.

ISBN-13: 978-0692312360 (Airship 27)
ISBN-10: 0692312366

Printed in the United States of America

10 9 8 7 6 5 4 3 2 1

VOLUME ONE

SATAN ON THE STUMP
BY JIM BEARD

Doctor Miles Murdock had been enjoying his dinner and the company of a beautiful woman until the sour-smelling hood in the cheap suit stuck a revolver in the surgeon's face.

The evening had begun earlier with light banter between Doc Murdock, one of the world's foremost plastic surgeons and his nurse, Dale Jordan. Dale had asked her boss if he'd care to accompany her to a fund-raising dinner at the local veteran's hall. Doc, assuming it to be a chance to contribute cash to a needy charity, was crestfallen to find that the dinner was to raise money for a political candidate.

Doc gave much of his own time and money to the less-fortunate of society by operating a clinic in the slums of Akelton City—he had little time and patience for politics and those who he perceived as striving to gain power for themselves on the backs of others. The candidate in question was S. J. Endermann and for Doc's comfort there were far too many questions about the man.

Still, Dale insisted he come with her to the dinner and offered to pay the entry fee for both of them. Doc, always a gentleman, allowed Dale's twinkling emerald eyes to win him over but would not let her pay for their dinners.

The young woman's beauty and resourcefulness often played havoc with Doc's feelings, but as long as he toiled at helping society in ways both public and covert he could not dream of marrying her. That would come only when he felt his work was done.

Later, despite being surrounded at the veterans hall by giant banners proclaiming "ENDERMANN FOR GOVERNOR," the meal was a pleasant affair made even more so by Dale's warm presence and only a short pre-dinner speech by the candidate.

Now, a gun pointed in his direction made Doc a bit uncomfortable.

"Okay, everybody," croaked the gunsel. "Stay in yer seats and nobody's gonna get hurt! We're here for the fat purse sittin' up at the front door and maybe a bit of jewelry…"

The man turned slightly to eyeball the crowd and his compatriots. Doc figured it to be six toughs in all, maybe more, each sporting a rod and an ugly scowl to match. A full house, he thought to himself. A small army of rats.

Dale shifted in her seat, anxiety washing over her face. Doc's attention swung to her, silently willing her to be still lest she attract the notice of the hood at their table. Unfortunately, the gunman noticed Dale and smiled evilly.

"Well, what we got here?" he said, pointing the gun at Dale. He looked her up and down, his large lips practically smacking at the sight of the girl in her form-fitting strapless gown and the string of pearls around her neck. "A little piece of fruit, ripe for the pickin'."

Doc made his move. Standing up suddenly, he reached for the hood's arm.

"Leave her alone, ugly!"

The gunsel did not take kindly to this interruption. Without taking his eyes off Dale, he lashed out and clubbed Doc across the temple with the barrel of his gun. Doc grunted and went down, hard. The other hoods laughed at the sight and went back to their gathering of booty from the diners. Better to let their comrade have a little fun and gather up what they could, they reasoned.

Dale screamed. The hood threw back his fleshy chin and barked out a laugh of his own. "Hey, Moxie and Karl!" he called out to the two goons at the next table. "Take the big bad hero here out and rough him up a little bit, eh? I gotta string o' pearls to take care of!"

On the floor, Doc grimaced but did not stir. Fully expecting the gunman's punch, he had rolled with the savage blow and dropped to make it look good. Hoping to somehow slip away in the confusion and chaos of the moment, now had a lot more on his plate to digest. The two goons grabbed him off the floor and roughly bundled him towards the door. Doc went as loose as possible, feigning unconsciousness.

Once outside the hall, the goons dropped Doc to the floor and stepping forward turned their backs to him. They then conferred over the beating to come.

Doc took the opportunity to stand up. He cleared his throat. The two men wheeled around and took in all six feet of Doc, his dark hair, solid form and piercing eyes. Eyes that now burned at them with a cold fire.

"Hey!" shouted one of the mugs. They both went for their guns but Doc sprang forward and taking a head in each hand soundly and roundly knocked them together. It was like a shot went off in the small, darkened entrance foyer. The men fell to the floor, dead still.

Doc grabbed both of their rods and leaped over the two gunmen. He made for the hall's coatroom and once there took a silent inventory. Finding his own coat, he slipped something from a deep inner pocket and then looking around purloined an opera cape and a dark slouch hat from another set of pegs. Setting his jaw, Doc tore from the room and located a stair well.

Hearing something behind him, he turned to see a lone figure run from the hall, through the foyer and out the door. It was S.J. Endermann himself. Doc cursed the politician's cowardice and turned back to the task before him.

Up he flew to a higher level, to a long balcony that stretched the entire length of the hall. In a darkened corner Doc drew out the object he had taken from his own coat and gazed at it. Made of gum rubber, it resembled a mask of sorts, one that's sickly violet hue seemed black in the shadows of his temporary hiding place. Doc stretched the mask up and over his head and fit it in place over his handsome features; his appearance changed from respected surgeon to walking corpse in an instant.

Only a few years before, Doc's brother, a well-loved Akelton policeman, was brutally murdered by criminals and his body left to rot underwater. Doc swore that day to war on all crime with every resource he could muster. Knowing that Doctor Miles Murdock could never make the impact on mobsters and gangsters he desired, he used his plastic surgery skills to fashion a hideous disguise which resembled his brother's corpse—this was the Purple Scar!

Placing the slouch hat on his head and whipping the cape around his shoulders, the Purple Scar moved to the balcony's railing and peering down into the hall assessed the situation.

Below, in the dining hall, the goons were still robbing the diners of their valuables. Their laughter grated on the Scar's ears. Spying Dale Jordan at her table, he saw the sour-smelling gunsel reaching for her. Whether the man was grasping for her necklace or the low neckline of her gown the Purple Scar did not know, only that he must act swiftly.

Knocking over a chair, he peered down into the hall again, hoping he had made enough noise.

The mook threatening Dale stopped suddenly and looked up. "Hey!" he grunted. "Someone's upstairs, on that balcony! Couple of you go and check it out!"

The Purple Scar smiled tightly under his mask; his distraction had worked perfectly. He then prepared to welcome his company.

Two of the gunman ran up a flight of stairs to the balcony, swinging their heads from left to right, looking for their prey. The Purple Scar stepped from the shadows and shot them both between the eyes.

The hall below erupted in chaos.

Women screamed and men bellowed; the criminals tried to discern what had just happened above them. Smelly aimed his gun at the balcony but was unable to draw a bead on their attacker. The Purple Scar had vanished as quickly as he had appeared.

Suddenly, the largest Endicott banner, which was hung across the entire balcony railing, was loosed from its perch and dropped to the floor below. The gigantic piece of canvas fell atop two of the goons and knocked them to the ground.

Smelly and his remaining compatriots opened fire on the balcony, filling the area with hot lead.

The Purple Scar evaded the gunfire by simply not being on the balcony. He flew down the stairs like a bat out of hell itself and met the criminals at the bottom with both feet. The impact made a sickening crunch. The Scar landed deftly and surveyed the scene. Dinner guests were running every which way, trying to avoid the gunplay and men in capes dropping on their heads. They were not the dark avenger's quarry, though. His attention he devoted to those who preyed upon them.

Down went a few more of the invaders under precise shots from the Purple Scar's revolvers. The room was now filled with smoke from unloading guns and coughing could be heard, as well as weeping. The Scar scanned the room for Smelly and spied him on the other side of a grouping of tables and patrons.

"Get out! Get out, you idiots!" Smelly cried at his comrades. "This ain't what we signed up for!"

The criminal turned to make a run for it but the Purple Scar was at his back and knocking him to the floor. Smelly then looked up into the barrel of the Scar's gun, pointing directly at his head.

"Your friends are either unconscious or dead," said the Purple Scar. "Regardless, this party seems to be finished. The police will soon be here—in fact, I think I hear their sirens now."

Smelly eyed his surroundings, saw that the diners had evacuated from the room and none of his comrades were coming to his rescue. It was just him and the grotesque figure pinning him to the ground and aiming between his eyes.

The Purple Scar's horrible visage came into full view then and the criminal recoiled at the sight of it. He tried to scrabble away but his entire body was stuck, as if pinned on a bug collector's board. Smelly's breath caught and he found it hard to draw another.

"*What did you think you were doing here?*" yelled the Purple Scar, only inches from his captive's face. "Why did you pick this place to rob? Who are you working for?"

Unable to breathe and feeling the walls closing in on him, Smelly felt a pain shoot up his arm and settle in his chest. The sickening features of the Purple Scar swam before his eyes.

Too well had Doctor Miles Murdock fashioned the mask to resemble his late brother's dead face. Too detailed were the mangled tissues, the rents and rivulets, the horrible scars left by the effect of John Murdock's body soaking in the river. Close up, the mask was every nightmare, every bogeyman in the shadows of a man's mind.

Smelly's heart gave out and he died.

The Purple Scar cursed under his breath when he saw the effects of his interrogation. Standing up, he listened and heard sirens growing closer.

Then he remembered Dale.

Praying his nurse had made it to safety, he mounted the stairs and flew back up to the balcony. Once again in the shadows, the Purple Scar ripped off his mask and stored it away in a pocket. The hat and cape he flung on the ground.

Doc Murdock began to walk down the back staircase, listening for sounds of the police's arrival. He could hear distraught partygoers outside the hall and then, finally, the squealing of brakes and the droning of sirens as Akelton's finest pulled up at the building. No doubt Captain Dan Griffin would be among them, he mused.

Dan Griffin had been John Murdock's best friend on the force, and the man who had imparted the bad news of John's murder to Doc. Once Doc had set himself on his course as the Purple Scar, he had let Griffin in on the secret and the police captain had become a kind of silent partner in the venture. His turning a blind eye on Doc's activities as the Scar had proved to be valuable in the avenger's war on criminals more than once.

Doc hoped that support was still in full force tonight.

Stepping outside, Doc fixed a confused look on his face and mussing up his hair a bit he stumbled towards the onrushing policemen. Dale appeared suddenly at his side and he looked at her with great relief. Before she could speak, Captain Dan Griffin stepped over to them, blocking their path.

"Mind telling me what's going on here, Doc?" said Griffin.

Doc looked up at him, somewhat sheepishly. He tried to catch Dale's eye but she was peering around at the other partygoers, all of whom wore varying expressions of fright and shock.

"It all happened so fast, Griff," said Doc. "Criminals crashed the dinner. Looking to steal Endermann's take for the evening, I guess. We all thought we were goners, until…"

"Until…?" queried Griffin.

Doc had to be careful with his words; though both Dale and Dan Griffin shared in the knowledge of his side-career as the Purple Scar, he couldn't be sure one or more of the partygoers clustered around them weren't inadvertently listening in.

"Well," said Doc. "It seems that the Purple Scar made another appearance tonight."

"Ah," Griffin said softly. "I see. Well, you and Dale run along—I'll let my men know I've already questioned you and that Miss Jordan was terribly shaken by the ordeal." He winked at the young woman. "I better find Mr. Endermann and insure him we'll be doing everything we can to provide more security for him and his people while they're in town campaigning."

Doc remembered seeing the gubernatorial candidate running for the door and smiled slightly at the thought. Dale blushed a bit and taking her arm, Doc nodded to Griffin and set off for their car. They paused when they heard the police captain begin to speak again.

"Thanks goodness the Purple Scar just happened to be in the area," he called to them.

"Yes," said Doc without turning. "Yes—thank goodness for the Purple Scar!"

+++

Despite the success of the previous evening, Doc Murdock rose with a curious sense of dread late the next morning.

Tommy Pedlar, the surgeon's valet and jack-of-all-trades, greeted him in the kitchen of his Swank Street mansion and without a word thrust a newspaper into Doc's hands.

He had planned to check in at his clinic in the slums after breakfast but his oppressive feeling only intensified after reading the daily newspaper's headline:

POLICE HUNT MYSTERY MAN IN FUNDRAISER ATTACK

Doc's eyes widened as he digested the words. They seemed unreal at first, but after reading them a second and than a third time the reality of the situation sunk in. The Purple Scar was a wanted man!

His mind whirled. Though he'd never operated in the open and his activities not exactly of an official nature, Doc had expanded his career as the Purple Scar with a keen sense of righteousness; hadn't he not only avenged his brother's death but continued to fight for justice in Akelton City? Hadn't he always tried to do what was right for its citizens?

Now, this dark day may have brought with it the beginning of the end for the Purple Scar!

"I can't believe it, Doc!" yelled Tommy. "But it's all there, in black 'n' white!"

Gaining control of his emotions, Doc forced himself to read the entire newspaper article. It wasn't a pretty picture.

The opening paragraph read:

Gubernatorial candidate S.J. Endermann called for a dragnet to bring in a man who escaped from last night's invasion of his fundraising dinner at Akelton City's veterans' hall. The popular politician told police at the scene that several criminal types had entered the hall and held his guests at gunpoint, with the intention of robbery and possibly murder. Endermann felt "very strongly" that one of the criminals attempted to double-cross the others and after slaying some of them escaped before police could apprehend the man.

Fury over Endermann's view of the events flooded over Doc. He had seen the man rush out of the hall before Doc had taken care of the mob of gunmen as the Purple Scar. What would he know of those events? He hadn't even been there!

The entire situation stank like yesterday's garbage.

The article sported a photo. It showed a small grouping of people standing outside the hall. They looked concerned, pensive. The caption below the photo explained who the people were:

(l to r) Mr. S.J. Endermann, his secretary Mr. Eric Boos, campaign manager Mr. Joseph Kowalski, bodyguard Mr. "Tiny" Thompson.

Doc knew precious little of Endermann before the fundraiser, save that the man was something of a controversial figure on the political scene. Though he had been in public office for many years now, if Doc remembered correctly, it was fairly recently he had caught the imagination of voters. Endermann was what the papers liked to call a "firebrand." And he was running for the office of state governor.

What was behind Endermann gunning for the Purple Scar? Doc's alter ego had never been actively hunted by law enforcement in Akelton, though, of course, his activities were hardly in line with official police procedures. Having Dan Griffin's approval, albeit silently, had helped the Scar seek justice beyond the scope of the law but he was only one man on a much larger force; maybe Doc's days as the dark avenger were now numbered with a figure such as Endermann, one who curried public favor to such a high degree, seeking to shut him down.

Doc thought then of witnessing the candidate's flight from the hall in the middle of the disturbance. He had branded the man a coward, someone unwilling to stand up for what he claimed to believe in and face adversity with a straight back. Perhaps there was something more to Endermann's actions last night. But if so, what?

And, now that he thought of it, where was "Tiny" Thompson, the bodyguard, when his boss was hightailing it away from the attack?

The surgeon turned to Tommy. "Please get Captain Griffin on the phone, would you? Tell him it's urgent—most likely he'll be expecting my call."

The thin, wiry man brightened. He completed the trio of people who knew that Doc Murdock and the Purple Scar were one and the same; Tommy felt certain that there was little that could stand in the way of his employer and the captain once they joined forces.

"Sure, Doc!" said Tommy. "And hey, don' forget, you got a lunch appointment today..."

"I'm going to have to disappoint Tony again, I'm afraid," said Doc. He'd been ducking a lunch engagement with an old friend for weeks, but there were larger concerns now; he wanted to talk to Dan Griffin as soon as possible, before Dale came in and he worried her unnecessarily.

Doc dressed for the day and entered his study. Tommy stuck his head in the door to inform him he had Detective-Captain Griffin of the Akelton Police Department, Homicide Division, on the line. The surgeon sat down at his desk and picked up the receiver.

"Griff?"

"Hi, Doc," came the reply. "Hold on sec."

Doc could hear the man get up and cross the floor, shut a door. In a moment, his friend was back on the phone.

"How bad is it?" queried Doc.

"Oh, you saw the headlines, eh?" said Griffin, ruefully. "It's bad. Pretty bad. The Purple Scar chose a poor time to swing into action."

"How bad is it?" Doc queried

Doc sighed. "Was anyone attending the dinner hurt?"

"No," chuckled the captain. "Just like you, Doc—always thinking of everyone else. But listen, the entire force is in a tizzy this morning. It started late last night when Endermann called the Commissioner. And you know how the Commissioner hates to be called out of bed. Anyway, Endermann's' blowin' a lot of hot air around and putting the thumbscrews on the top brass. He wants you…err, the Purple Scar in the worst way."

"But why, Griff?" spat Doc. "Why would a candidate for governor, a man who before last night probably didn't even know the Scar existed, want his head? Hadn't I saved his money, not to mention all his very wealthy guests?"

"Endermann's got the entire election in the bag," said Griffin, quietly. "Or so he thinks. And so the polls say, too. He's come out nowhere—practically—and he's been making a lot of noise about 'the sanctity of law' and 'respect for authority' at every stop he's made throughout the state. People seem to like him. My guess he's looking to make that one, big score, right before the election, to sew the whole thing up. What better than to return, the prodigal son, and clean up your hometown."

"Hometown?"

"Doc, Endermann's from Akelton. Didn't you know?"

The surgeon's mind raced. Instead of becoming clearer, the entire thing was making less sense, if that were possible. "No," he said, finally. "No, I didn't know."

The captain continued. "Speaking of money, the thing is, and this is just scuttlebutt, they say he's hurting. And I don't mean his campaign. That's got plenty of lettuce. It's him. Endermann. Word is that his personal finances are one big red slash."

"That's very interesting," said Doc, chewing on the thought. "Are you suggesting Endermann was somehow behind the attack on the veteran's hall?"

"I'm not saying he was…or that he *wasn't*."

"Wait, you have some of the gunman from last night in custody, don't you? I didn't kill all of them."

Griffin chuckled again, but coldly. "Yeah, we have a few of them. But they haven't told us much, just that they had heard the purse was going to be a fat one at the fundraiser and being a needy cause themselves, thought they'd grab it up. Why do you ask?"

Silence came over the line and the captain guessed Doc was thinking. "Griff, one of those mugs said something in the middle of it, when things started to go downhill for them. He said, 'this ain't what we signed up for...' To me, that sounds like someone put them up to it, promised them easy pickings and a cut of the action."

"Say, you may have something there!" Griffin enthused. "But its pretty thin evidence to pin it all on Endermann—as much as I'd like to. That guy just rubs me the wrong way."

Doc grit his teeth. "Sounds like I may need to look into this—or rather, the Purple Scar does."

"Listen, Doc," said Griffin, trying to keep his voice calm. "I...I can't help you. This, this runs *deep*, you understand? This may be the deepest, tightest corner you've ever gotten yourself into. Endermann's got everyone in his pocket and every Tom, Dick and Harry joining in the manhunt. He's got the papers and the radio stations primed with enough explosives to blow the whole city wide open. My boss has me under pretty tight wraps—no, I don't mean he suspects any ties to the Scar—but as chief of Homicide I'm expected to toe the line and mobilize my men to help bring in the 'mystery man.' The Purple Scar is now officially a murderer. And a very, very wanted man.

"You're on your own. I'm sorry."

Doc smiled. Dan Griffin was a good man. His late brother John spoke so highly of him, before he was murdered in cold blood by loathsome criminals. Griffin was only doing his job. Doc couldn't expect much more.

But maybe he could still ask a single, small favor.

"Griff, do one thing for me, eh? Get me the mugshots of one of the goons from last night, and any other information you've got on him." Doc paused. "Can you do that?"

"Doc, that I can do."

"Good," said Doc. "I'll send Tommy over to pick them up. Thanks, Dan. John would be very proud of you. Good bye—and happy hunting!"

"Same to you, boy! Same to you!"

Setting the receiver down, Doc didn't waste another minute but called Tommy into the room. He looked squarely at his helper, and remembered that John had thought very highly of Tommy, too.

"I need you to run down to police headquarters and pick something up for me from Captain Griffin," Doc placed a hand on the smaller man's shoulder. "And there's another thing, too."

"Anything, Doc," said Tommy, enthusiastically. "I owe you a lot!"

Doc smiled, then allowed a more serious expression to shift into place on his face. "I need you to dig up some information on S. J. Endermann.

Pull in every favor you're owed on the streets, Tommy. I don't want rumors or hearsay—I need the real dirt on the man. I need to know if he's hiding anything. And what he's afraid of."

Tommy, once the accomplished pickpocket known as the Sticky-Fingered Kid, grinned with a devilish gleam in his eye. "Sure, Doc. No sweat. It'll be tough, but I'll come through for you!"

The surgeon watched him go and then turned back to his desk. He had much to ponder and plan for. Let Endermann try and find him, he thought. He'd find the Purple Scar a constituent to be reckoned with.

+++

S.J. Endermann was in a highly agitated state.

His voice rang through the rooms and hallways of his temporary headquarters just outside Akelton City. The stately mansion and its surrounding acres were loaned to him by the mayor and the candidate had been occupying the house for some weeks now.

"The new poll results are unacceptable," he bellowed at his campaign manager. "By God, Kowalski, we can't afford any miss-steps at this juncture!"

The rotund little man leaned back in his chair and unable to meet the politician's eyes looked down at his shoes.

"One wonders," he began, "if it was prudent to start this search for, well, this 'vigilante.'"

Endermann's face flushed from his burly moustache up to his forehead. "Get out!" he cried. "And don't come back until you've got better numbers! And tell my secretary to get in here!"

Kowalski left, gladly, and Endermann's secretary entered. The prissy little man was able to look his boss in the eye, unlike the campaign manager.

"Hold all my calls, Eric," said Endermann. "I don't wish to be disturbed for the next hour. Let Thompson know, too."

Eric Boos gave a curt nod and raising one eyebrow slightly turned on his heel and exited, shutting the double oak doors of the library behind him. The candidate seemed to relax slightly and then rose from his chair. He walked to the windows and pulled down the blinds of each of them in turn, as well as closing their heavy curtains. When the room was significantly darkened he returned to his chair and reseated himself.

A minute passed. Then another. Finally, a voice spoke.

"Those hired men were idiots. Complete bunglers."

"Agreed," said Endermann.

"Unfortunately, some of them still live."

The candidate shifted in his seat. The room's darkness permeated every corner, every inch of floor and ceiling. "I feel certain all roads back to me are sufficiently washed out. I haven't come this far by being incautious."

"*We* haven't come this far, Endermann," said the voice. "Never forget that. We've come far *together*. But, *you* are now in deep debt and it grows deeper every day. Your campaign is entirely solvent, but you, my friend, are *not*. We cannot touch your campaign coffers. That would be too risky. All that was raised at the dinner last night could have easily solved your problems."

"*My* problems?" Endermann thundered. "You make much of our shared venture save for when *my* proclivities drain the bankbook!"

"Yes, yes," soothed the voice. "Let us look past that point for now—the matter at hand is that we need a *crisis*. The election is only two weeks from now. Your victory, though you may feel otherwise, is not a certainty. I can see too many variables—your debts being chief among them. If anyone would uncover them…"

Endermann stroked his chin, tousled his moustache. Though in his sixth decade he was not an un-handsome man. He knew full well what a striking, charismatic figure he cut.

"Yes, damn you, I know. I will admit this gambit against the Akelton vigilante is a good one, one that could cover a multitude of sins, but it also makes me nervous. We've campaigned on the virtues of law and the like but we've never bothered to, you know, actually *fight crime*."

The voice tittered, an unholy sound in the darkness. "How does one truly fight one's self? Once this 'hero' is caught and hung out to dry, you can claim it as another of your successes—and your victory in the election will be secured. Then, after you are in office, it won't matter what skeletons are in your closet. You will be governor. And then, someday, President of the United States.

"You are the *face*, though, Endermann. Never forget that. You are the mouthpiece and I am the speaker. My work runs much deeper than yours. You are a necessary evil, something I must endure to achieve my goals. You must always remember that."

Endermann grimaced. "Yes, you are right. I had virtually nothing before you…approached me. An alderman, a council member, a cipher in a greater political machine. Now, our power grows and everything I have hoped for is coming true. People are sheep. I have always known this. All they need is someone to lead them, and someone to keep them in line. Someone like me."

"Like *us*," said the voice.

"Yes," answered the candidate in the darkened room. "Yes, like us."

"Now," breathed the voice, barely a whisper. "Marshal our forces and let us trap this fly in our web. And once we have him, into The Room he shall go. There, we will flay him and dissect him and see what makes him tick… and then hang him out for all to see."

✝✝✝

With mugshots in hand, Doc Murdock retired to his studio on the top floor of his Swank Street mansion. There, surrounded by half-finished sculptures and busts of clay and wax, he laid out the photos of the gunman currently in police custody.

The surgeon's hands worked feverishly on a bust. When he was done, Doc stepped back and looked approvingly at his work. Then, he set a small mirror in front of him and began to apply the fruits of his labors to his own face.

Once finished, he twisted the dial on a wall safe and listening for the tumblers to click into place he twisted the handle and opened it. Doc reached inside and took out the mask of the Purple Scar. Securing it in a secret inner pocket of his coat he then removed a revolver and that too disappeared into his coat.

Lastly, he placed his hand on a small picture of his brother. For a long moment, the surgeon looked at it and then placed it back into the safe.

Doc walked to a rear door of his house, one that led to an old, unused alley, and paused before a full-length mirror that hung nearby. Looking into he saw not Doctor Miles Murdock but the gunman who had shattered his night out on the town with Dale.

"Let's go pay a call on our benefactor, shall we?" he said and stepped through the door.

✝✝✝

Having parked his car a fair pitch down the road, Doc Murdock walked to S.J. Endermann's borrowed mansion on the outskirts of town. Storm clouds roiled and rumbled in the distance.

Now disguised as Moxie Mahr, one of the gunsels who invaded the veterans' hall, Doc knew it wouldn't do to be seen driving his own expensive roadster. Better to fill the role completely if he were to gain entrance to Endermann's conclave and pierce the mystery at hand.

Before he had left his Swank Street home, the surgeon had pored over the dossier on Mahr that Dan Griffin had sent along with the man's mugshots. The file contained not only notes from Mahr's interrogation but a lot of dirt on his past run-ins with the law. Overall, Doc knew more about the man whose face he now wore than Endicott himself. Other than a few newspaper clippings from the past few years, there was little to go on concerning the candidate—Doc hoped fervently that Tommy Pedlar could unearth a few nuggets to add to the Purple Scar's meager arsenal.

As he approached the outer gate of the Mansion, Doc could not shake the feeling deep in his gut that Endermann was behind the attack of the night before. He had no real concrete evidence but he knew by now never to ignore such a deep-seated warning bell from his intuition. Endermann was a phony and subverting the trust of the people who'd put him in office, thought Doc with conviction, but the man's political standing and the highest seat in the state currently within arm's reach would make bringing him down one of the Purple Scar's greatest challenges.

Doc was up for that battle. He hoped his disguise as Moxie Mahr would pass muster.

Men who appeared to be guards stood outside the gate to the sprawling house. Doc could see they were armed. If he didn't get past them the entire gambit was a wash. He rounded his shoulders, flipped up the collar of his old suit coat and shuffled into view.

"Okay, stop right there, buddy," announced one of the men, eyeing Doc's worn clothes. "I think you got the wrong place."

Doc grinned. "I'm here to see Endermann. Tell 'im Moxie Mahr wants a word with 'im."

Another man stepped over. He was as big as a barn and mean-looking. Doc recognized him as "Tiny" Thompson, Endicott's personal bodyguard.

"Hiya, boys. What's going on?" Thompson also looked Doc up and down, clearly not liking what he saw.

The disguised surgeon felt a pivot point in his mission had arrived. He took a leap of faith.

"Hello, Thompson," he spat. "I think your boss will want t'see me, don't ya think?"

The hulking bodyguard frowned at Doc's words. A cloud passed over his face. A moment passed and then he spoke.

"Yeah, let 'im in. I'll take him up to the house myself."

The guards unlatched the heavy gate and swung it open. One of them gave a mocking bow to Doc and silently bid him to enter. Doc shuffled past him without a word and fell in next to Thompson.

The big man motioned for Doc to raise his arms and he was soon divested of his revolver. Knowing full well that there was a distinct possibility of being disarmed before entering Endermann's camp did not soften the blow.

Incredibly, the bodyguard said nothing while they walked up the drive to the mansion, though the surgeon could feel the man's eyes on him, scrutinizing. He prayed his disguise was good enough. Thompson was no dummy, of that he was now certain.

Doc was taken in a side door and down a hallway to a room at the front of the house. From what he had seen so far, the entire place was sumptuously decorated—someone had a rich appetite for the good things in life. The room he was ushered into was set up as a kind of office, with an immense desk of oak and an entire battalion of file cabinets. Campaign signs and other Endermann propaganda littered every corner.

There were three men in the room. Off to one side, Doc saw Boos the secretary conferring with Kowalski the campaign manager. Behind the desk sat S.J. Endermann.

"What can we do for you, Mr...?" asked the candidate. He didn't offer his hand, nor did he stand up.

Doc took another leap. "You owe me money, Endermann."

The politician arched an eyebrow. He looked perplexed.

"I do? And for what, may I ask?"

Something was wrong. Doc was getting strange signals from the man, almost as if he truly didn't know who Mahr was. Almost.

He glanced over at Boos and Kowalski. They were both frowning. The secretary look at Thompson and Doc felt as if something passed between the two men, silently.

"For a deal gone sour," answered Doc, pressing ahead. "Me and the boys were hired to snatch that fat purse at your little shindig, but all we got was a beat-down and a trip to the pokey with some bluecoats...and some of us're dead!"

The air in the room shifted again. To Doc's surprise, Thompson stepped forward and spoke. "What happened?" he growled.

"The Purple Scar!" yelped Doc. "The Purple Scar's what happened!"

"Explain yourself," said Boos.

Doc swallowed. Time to lay it on thick. "We got there and everythin' seemed t'be goin' swell, but then this mug appears out of *nowhere* and next thing I know some o' my pals are bleedin' on the floor! This guy is a real hellcat—we're droppin' like flies, see! Next thing I know the cops are there and I'm in jail!"

"In jail?" asked Thompson. "How did you get out?"

Doc looked right at the bodyguard. "They let me go! Questioned me and then told me t'scram! Queerest thing I ever seen!"

The room grew silent, the air thick. Doc looked at all four men in turn, ending up on Endermann.

"Now I want what's owed me!"

"Get rid of him," whispered Endermann, finally. A lone bead of sweat trickled down his forehead.

Thompson grabbed Doc by the arms so fast the surgeon had little chance to react. He cursed himself for not recognizing where the situation was heading. Now, he had bigger troubles.

With Doc's arms in a viselike grip, the bodyguard strong-armed the disguised surgeon out of the room and down the hall in the blink of an eye. For a big man he was lightning fast. Doc's mind whirled and scrambled to react.

Two other men, both rough-looking types, materialized out of doorways and each taking an arm from Thompson frog-marched Doc out a door and into the open air.

Doc looked around and saw he was in a courtyard of some sort. He spied no other doors into the area save the one they just came through, but he noticed the surrounding roof was low here, low enough for a man to reach up and grab its eaves.

Then, he heard a gun being cocked behind his right ear.

"Take him out to the gully when you're done with him," said Thompson. He turned without further adieu and closed the door behind him.

One of the men told Doc to get on his knees, facing away from them, and to interlace his hands on top of his head.

A drop of rain touched his cheek, and then another. The sky rumbled and darkened. "Let's get this over with," said one of the men. "I don't wanna get wet."

Doc began to drop to one knee but then suddenly jabbed backwards with a foot and caught one of the men hard in the ankle. He could hear something snap and the man went down, bellowing and cursing.

Wasting not a precious second, Doc took advantage of the other man's surprise and drove a fist into his gut. The gunsel doubled over, air exploding loudly from him. Doc deftly caught his gun and swiftly placing its mouth on the man's temple, pulled the trigger.

Swinging around, he did the same to the man with the broken ankle.

Doc ran for the low-hanging eaves of the roof and hoped the noise of his actions was minimal. That hope died when the door to the courtyard flew open and Thompson's gargantuan form filled its frame.

Gunfire bloomed around him as he caught the nearest gutter and pulled himself up. Luckily, the roof's shingles were in good repair and did not loosen as Doc scrambled onto the incline and made his way to the peak. He could hear Thompson's yell when he saw his men dead on the ground and still more bullets tore at his clothes and the roof around him.

Doc threw himself over the peak of the roof and landing on the other side paused a moment to catch his breath. A few more shots whizzed over his head and then stopped. Doc listened and heard the gutters on the other side creak and groan under someone's weight. Thompson screamed for other men to join him in the pursuit.

The surgeon let go and allowed himself to slide down the roof to whatever waited below.

Doc dropped to the ground and quickly took in his surroundings. He guessed he was at the back of the house. The rain pelted him and he swore under his breath; not a very good situation to be in. Unarmed and hunted in a strange place, his options were slim. And to make matters worse, his disguise was melting under the deluge.

Hearing sounds of pursuit to the left, he ran to the right. He followed the outer wall of the house until he came to an area of dense trees and shrubbery that hugged the structure and offered sanctuary. Doc fell to his stomach and crawled underneath the thick growth and out of sight.

Wanting to distance himself even further from his hunters, the surgeon crawled deeper into the foliage. Moving past a window, he heard voices coming from inside. Weighing the immediate danger, Doc allowed himself a moment to listen.

It was Endermann, talking to someone.

"…could I have done?" yelled the candidate. "I felt it was wise to dispatch the man!"

"How can we be sure he was who he said he was?" asked the other. "The police just don't let criminals go like that—I suspect it was a trap of some sort."

Doc didn't recognize the voice. Low and gravelly, it almost sounded to the surgeon's experienced ears as if someone were disguising their own true voice.

"What do you make of this Purple Scar business?" Endermann queried.

"Our mystery man of the other night. Akelton's protector. There were rumors of such a figure but I dismissed it as a tall tale among the lowlifes and criminal element. I give it much more credence now."

Straining to get closer to the window to peer inside, Doc was held back by a low-hanging branch of a large tree. It prevented him from gaining a solid view of the room and its occupants. All he could see was that it was very dark in the room.

"I cannot be exposed, Endermann," said the voice, plaintively. "This entire production will crumble and our chances of you sitting in the governor's seat dashed. This man must be captured and killed. We cannot afford to waste any more time on this—the bank could call in those notes at any moment and your entire political career ruined forever."

Before Doc could hear Endermann's response, a hound bayed nearby. Too close, he thought. Flight was now the only option.

He crawled away from the window and the house, his mind trying to digest all that he had heard. It was now a fact that Endermann was behind the attack at the fundraiser and was in some sort of personal financial trouble. It explained his need for money but it didn't explain his bloodthirstiness. Who was the mysterious other who drove him to murder?

Both Boos and Kowalski were contenders. It was evident they were well-positioned cogs in Endermann's political machine. Thompson, too, was a suspect, he supposed. But regardless of who it was, what did the gain by operating in this manner?

Doc reached a fence after scrabbling for yards under the brush and trees. Guessing it was the border of Endermann's borrowed property, he smashed a lower slat of the wooden barrier and pulled himself through it and to the other side. There, he found a small dirt road that led off into the distance, away from the mansion.

When he had recovered his car and was sure he wasn't being followed, Doc Murdock allowed himself to mull over the entire tale once again.

R.J. Endermann was definitely not someone who deserved the public's trust and support. The man deserved to be in prison—or strapped into the electric chair.

It was up to the Purple Scar to stop him. But how?

Doc made up his mind to return to the mansion later that night as his frightening alter-ego. Despite the manhunt for the Purple Scar, despite the danger, he had to bring this story to an immediate close. With the election looming on the horizon and Endermann seemingly fooling the great majority of the voting public, time was of the essence.

He would do whatever was necessary to end the candidate's winning streak—for good.

+++

The rain had finally let up, and Doc Murdock sat in his study at his Swank Street home. He had a lot to think about.

A man had come to Akelton under the guise of a righteous crusader for the public good, a politician whose meteoric rise seemed to grab people's imagination and give them hope. But it was a sham. S.J. Endermann, the favorite son of Akelton, had secrets and those secrets made him a very dangerous character indeed.

Doc couldn't fathom the whys and hows; Tommy Pedlar had yet to return from his fact-finding mission and the surgeon knew that key components to the mystery had yet to be revealed. Endermann had an accessory, someone who perhaps even called the shots and orchestrated the candidate's entire scheme against the people of the state. The mysterious voice he'd heard in the room at Endermann's headquarters might be one of his employees, posing as a string-puller, or it might still be another, yet unknown, personage.

It was a mystery, but Doc felt he had little time to ponder it. He must act, and act swiftly. The election loomed.

Wrapping up his current work at his office and his clinic, Doc dressed in dark clothes and outfitted himself with a revolver, a flashlight, a set of special keys and the mask of the Purple Scar.

Driving once again towards Endermann's mansion, the surgeon kept close watch on the streets he crossed, staying alert for police. Captain Dan Griffin's men would be out looking for the Purple Scar and he wasn't keen on giving them what they wanted.

Letting Griffin in on his plan at this critical juncture would do no good either; the Scar was on his own.

Once near the mansion, he secured his roadster and hoofed it over to the main gate. Standing back, the Scar hid himself in the shadows and watched. The gate was manned, of course, and with more guards than earlier in the day. He was expected, perhaps.

Suddenly, "Tiny" Thompson stepped into view. The burly bodyguard spoke to the men at the gate and they shared some joke or humorous story. Their laughter broke the night and then quieted. The Scar then watched as

Thompson walked away, back towards the house.

Following the big man with his eyes, the Scar slipped silently along the outside wall of the house's grounds, trying to keep pace with Thompson. The bodyguard stopped to light a cigarette and the dark avenger made his move. Scaling the wall, he perched like a gargoyle at its top and, verifying that no one else was in sight or earshot, he snapped a twig he'd brought with him.

Thompson's head whirled around. He made for the wall.

The Scar dropped on him like a lead weight. Both went down yet only one arose: the Purple Scar.

He made for the outer door he was taken through on his previous visit, calling up a mental picture of the house's layout. The Scar took out his set of keys and began to work on the lock. This was a unique set of keys, loaned to him by Tommy Pedlar; they were the stock in trade of the thief. They held the rich promise of getting through any locked door or portal.

Slipping inside the great house, the Scar flitted down a hallway and tried to recall the way to the room in which he had encountered Endermann, Boos and Kowalski. He pulled up short when voices came to his ears from down the passageway. The Scar peered around a corner and witnessed a strange tableau.

One of a set of massive double doors opened into a cross corridor and two men exited with a woman between them. They held her arms. She walked as if her clothes had been heavily starched. Her mouth was a tight slit, her jaw stone. Her eyes were open, yet dead.

The Scar recognized the woman as the head of the Akelton Public School Board. She had strong opinions and he recalled that those opinions often riled local politicians. But, the woman was popular among parents and others.

"That's right, Dolly," said one of the men, quietly, in her ear. "You go home now and sleep. In the morning, you'll feel better."

"Yes," spoke the other, smiling like a cobra. "You'll see things in a different light."

The woman simply nodded once and they escorted her down the hallway and through another door.

Intrigued, the Purple Scar stepped silently up to the double doors and placed a palm on one. The need to know what lay beyond them burned within him; they might yield a solution to the entire mystery.

He utilized Tommy's keys and the lock gave way. Opening the door he slipped inside. Darkness engulfed him. Believing he'd heard a noise in

The Scar dropped on him like a lead weight

the corridor, the Scar shut the door behind him, quietly. Now, he stood in absolute blackness.

The room's shadows would offer no answers until he dispelled them. The Scar pulled out his torch and activated it. No light sprung forth. Cursing under his breath, he felt along its length and to its aperture. He realized then it had probably been broken when he landed on Thompson outside.

When he had first entered, the scant light of the corridor had given him a fleeting image of a medium-sized parlor. In its center, a scattering of furniture stood. Disturbingly, a small clutch of people seemed to occupy the chairs and sofas; if this were true, they said nothing and remained seated. The Scar turned to the doors.

Before he could reach for the door handle, the sound of a heavy bolt sliding into place resounded through the space. It chilled him to the bone. The Purple Scar was trapped.

✛✛✛

"Welcome," said a voice. It resembled that which spoke with Endermann earlier. "I must admit, I never imagined we'd catch you so handily. We barely had to do a thing—and here you are."

The Scar again could not place the voice. He was now certain, though, that it was affected; someone was concealing their true identity. It couldn't be Thompson—or could it? Hadn't he made sure the bodyguard was out for the count? But then again, who else could have followed him here, waited for him to enter the room?

"I can tell what you're thinking," announced the voice. "But that isn't pertinent at the moment. *Your* identity is. Who are you?"

"I much prefer talking about *you*," said the Scar. He reached out a hand and brushed the top of the head of the person sitting nearest him. A department store mannequin. "Your stranglehold on the election—and this city—is temporary. You won't get away with pulling the wool over everyone's eyes. I can't imagine why Endermann would be so blind himself to ally himself with you."

The voice chuckled, low and devilishly. "Endermann! He's a means to an end, I suppose; a necessary evil. *I* hold the true power, my friend. I pull the strings. He'd be nobody without me. He'd be a wanderer in the darkness—just like you, at this moment."

Darkness had never bothered the Scar, but he grew concerned that in this room it would not be to his benefit. He regretted not bringing matches.

"This is all of little concern to someone whose own game has come to an end. The great Akelton avenger, its dark knight, caught like a fly in a web—and after your bungled attempt at invading this house this afternoon. Yes, we realize now that it was you, in disguise. Now, tell me who you really are!"

The Purple Scar laughed low in his throat. "Sorry. Not interested."

Suddenly, the room flared with light! Hot, exploding light, which filled the space completely and burned at his retinas. He cried out, and as swiftly as the illumination came, it expired.

Balls of light danced before his eyes and he ground his palms against them. There was nothing he could do; he was sure he was nearly blinded.

Then, something sharp punctured his left calf. The Scar jumped back and bumped into a piece of furniture. He grasped at his leg but felt nothing save a sore spot on the muscle of his calf.

"Now," said the voice. "Let us discuss a few things."

His head swam. Perspiration broke out across his body. The floor seemed to curve, then buckle. Everything tilted. Had he been drugged?

Across the room, a large symbol appeared on the wall, as if fading in from nothing. A spiraling shape, it glowed with cold fire, barely illuminating the surroundings but for some reason the Scar could not tear his eyes from it.

It began to revolve, slowly.

"WHO ARE YOU?" boomed the voice. It seemed to come from everywhere, deafening in its volume.

Almost blind, drugged and unable to look away from the hypnotic pull of the revolving symbol, the Scar fought to remain on his feet. His stomach lurched. His brain felt like mush.

"WHO ARE YOU?" the voice exploded again.

The dark avenger held his head in his hands, barely able to think. His mind fled backwards in time, to his days in school, training to be a physician. What drug would they have used? How could he fight this?

"YOU ARE NOTHING!" spat the voice, its mocking tones filling the room. "One lowly man, pathetically scrabbling to bring 'justice' to the world. I repeat: you are *nothing*!"

Why couldn't he close his eyes? Why did he himself spin with the spiral shape on the wall? Could…could what the voice said possibly be true?

Doctor Miles Murdock looked at himself and saw…what? A surgeon who took the law into his own hands when it had failed to protect his brother. A vigilante. A desperate man who sought…vengeance? And how? By wearing a face of horror. By wearing the face of his brother's hideously scarred corpse.

What *was* he doing?

"I sense you seek something," said the voice. "A man does not simply operate outside the law on a whim. There is something you want, you *need*. We can *help* you. We have many means at our disposal. You only have to *trust* us."

The Purple Scar weakly nodded. The shape on the wall continued to spiral downward, downward. His knees buckled but he did not fall.

"You *must* trust us. Tell us who you are and we *will* help you."

Think! The Scar tried to *think*. But the noise and the light and the warm sensation creeping up his leg and spreading through his body conspired to cloud his mind.

"TELL US WHO YOU ARE!"

No, he thought. No, he was a good man. That was right, wasn't it? This place housed *evil*, and neither the police nor the Mayor nor the city council nor anyone in Akelton could do anything about it! But *he* could. He alone could...wasn't that right?

If only he could *think*.

Remorse for his brother John flooded over him. A vision of Dale Jordan flitted before his eyes. So beautiful. John, so horrifyingly dead. Dale, Dale... why couldn't he love her? Why did John stand in his way?

In the dim light from the glowing symbol, he saw the mannequins turn towards him, their accusing eyes piercing him through. They all frowned.

Wasn't it Dale that he fought for? And Tommy Pedlar? And Tommy's sickly daughter? And Dan Griffin? Wasn't it the innocents for whom he became the Purple Scar?

And the woman from the School Board. She was lost. She'd been subjugated. She...

Grief and shame washed over him. He screamed and crumpled to the floor.

After many long minutes the lights came up in the room. On the floor lay the Purple Scar in a crumpled mass, face down. He did not stir.

The double doors were unlatched from the outside and then they opened. Two men marched in and approached the form of the unconscious man. Leaning over him, the one grasped a shoulder and rolled him over.

There, in the full light of the room, was the face of the Purple Scar.

The man gasped. The other yelped. The Scar kicked out and caught one of them in the kneecap. He drove a hard fist into the face of the man who bent over him. Both went down. The Scar scrambled to his feet and pulled out his revolver.

He glanced up to see a high ceiling and what appeared to be curtained windows far up on the walls, a story above the floor. It reminded him of an operating theater. He surmised that the flash of light would have come from that vicinity—and the voice.

He drew his aim on the windows and pumped lead into them. The glass shattered under the onslaught of slugs and the curtains danced.

One of the men on the floor suddenly grabbed his leg. It was the one in which he received the hallucinatory drug; it stung like hell when the man grabbed it. The Scar kicked out and caught his assailant on the chin, sending him rolling into a heap a few feet away. He wheeled around when he heard the cocking of a gun behind him and caught the other man in the forehead with a blast from his own revolver.

Wasting no further time, the dark avenger sped towards the double doors and into the corridor. A door opened on the other end and deposited Joe Kowalski, the campaign manager. The Scar could see what looked like a staircase behind the man. Kowalski saw the Scar and alarm filled his face.

"What…what the *hell*?"

Kowalski drew a piece and began to raise it to fire. He didn't get far as blood fountained from his chest, just over his heart. The aim of the Purple Scar, even under duress, was true.

More men seemed to appear all around him then, and he dove and twisted to avoid their gunfire. The hallways quickly filled with the booming sound of blasting shots and the smell of gunpowder. Men screamed. Some died.

There were still many questions left unanswered, but the Purple Scar was drained and thought only of escaping the wretched mansion with his life. He unloaded his revolver carefully, never wasting a bullet when he could avoid it but always shooting to kill when he found himself in another's crosshairs. Sweat poured out from under his gum elastic mask and his clothes were soaked by the time he once again found the outdoors.

He ran at a fever pitch across the grounds and towards the wall. At that moment he reached the barrier, he remembered Thompson the bodyguard. And then, like a ghost, the giant of a man was in front of him, a police special in his hand and aiming to kill.

The Scar went low and slid along the slick grass like a baseball player sliding into home. The move seemed to take Thompson by surprise. So did the hole that appeared in his sternum. When it gushed thick red blood, the bodyguard's surprise only grew. Then, he toppled over and lay still.

Up and over the wall, the Scar did not devote time to his deed. He dragged himself along, thinking only of reaching his roadster and to drive far, far away from this place.

+++

Captain Dan Griffin sat at his desk in his office at Police Headquarters and sighed. Running his hands through his graying hair, he was sure things had never smelled this rotten before. The next few days looked pretty grim from his point of view.

A knock at his door caused the captain to look up. There in the doorway stood Doctor Miles Murdock. He looked like at least ten miles of bad road, thought Griffin.

"Hiya, Dan," said the surgeon with a slight smile. "Mind if I sit down?"

Griffin pointed to a chair as he crossed the room to shut his door. He turned to his friend, face reddening.

"What did you *do*, Doc? I never seen it this bad before!"

Doc chuckled softly and shook his head. "Sit down, Dan, and I'll tell you what I know."

He told him of his visit to Endermann's mansion, of the School Board leader and his own peril in the madness room. He also told him of his escape.

"Sounds like one of the tightest scrapes you've ever been in," said Griffin, eyes wide.

"Quite possibly," replied Doc. "And you know what kind of situations I usually get into. I thought I was a goner then, but when I conjured up the face of my friends, of the woman they had already brainwashed, well, something came surging through me. It was enough to regain my wits. I acted as if they had me, so as to fool them into lowering their guard."

"You're a lucky, lucky man, Doc…and a damn foolish one. Endermann's completely blown his stack this time. He wants the Purple Scar's head and he wants it yesterday. Wants this whole situation wrapped up before the election…"

The surgeon looked up suddenly, concern creasing his brow. "That's the day after tomorrow, isn't it?"

"Yep," said Griffin, forlorn.

"Listen, Griff—you've got to go out to his place and arrest Endermann. He has to be stopped. There's a lot that I haven't figured out yet, but he's sitting on a nest of murderers and traitors…"

"Boy, you just don't get it, do you?" yelled the captain. "Doc, I have *nothing* on Endermann. *He's* got plenty on the Scar. He says our local mystery man came to his place and murdered his people and tried to blow up the whole shooting match. Now –"

Came another knock at the door and both men looked up to see a police sergeant with Tommy Pedlar in tow. The sergeant did not look happy.

"Says he wants to talk to you, Cap'n," announced the man.

Griffin glanced at Doc, who nodded solemnly. The captain motioned for Tommy to come in and to shut the door behind him.

"Tommy, I hate to place this weight on you," began Doc. "But what you have to tell us may be the solving of this entire case."

The former thief took in his surroundings. "Boy, you don't make this easy on a guy, do ya, Doc?"

The little man leaned in towards the other two and spoke quietly.

"I been deep, Doc. Maybe deeper 'en I ever been before. And I seen dirt like I ain't never seen. This guy Endermann, well, he's a bad man. He's got debts like you wouldn't believe and a lot of spooky characters on his payroll. One old so-and so I talked to said he'd been cheated so bad by Endicott he thought he'd like to croak him himself."

"What kind of debts, Tommy?" asked Doc.

"Gamblin', mostly," said the former Sticky-Fingered Kid. "Maybe some other stuff, but he likes the horses and he don' win so much. Funny, 'cause he always goes on and on about living a clean life and how we should turn our backs on the stuff that tempts us. You know, real preachy-like."

Doc glanced at Griffin. "This sound anything like the high and mighty S.J. Endermann you know?"

"Nossir," said the captain. "I envy the Purple Scar like you wouldn't believe. To get my hands around that guy's neck…"

"I almost felt sorry for him at first, when I started diggin' down through his story," Tommy announced. "Guy had a bad turn, the kind a lot of people don' come back from."

"Bad turn?" asked Doc.

"Yeah, his old lady was killed in an accident, 'bout ten years ago or so. Endermann was drivin' them to a show, I heard, and another guy cut 'em off and they hit a pole. Wife didn't last much more'n hour after that."

Griffin and Doc looked at each other, a bit thunderstruck.

"Let me lay this out, boys," said Griffin. "Endermann's a pipsqueak, a nobody who got elected to the Akelton city council and didn't make so much as a little ripple in the pond. Then, his wife is killed and he—what? Suddenly starts wowin' 'em at the voting booth?"

"That's probably why I don't really remember him," Doc said, thoughtful. "A minor politician whose star didn't really start to rise until he went to the state capital."

"Right, right!" enthused Tommy. "That's how I got it. Things started happenin' for him after his wife croaked and he put all these people in place around 'im—like a whole crowd of pencil-pushers and number-crunchers and the like. Got himself a machine that runs real smooth. "

Doc clamped a hand on his valet's shoulder. "Tommy, this is fantastic. You've done quite a job. Now, if I could just figure out who his partner in this mess is."

"Say," said Tommy. "I got one more thing: after the accident, he used'ta go to one of those witch doctors, whattaya call 'em? Sigh...sigh-ki-o..."

"A psychiatrist?" offered Doc.

"Yeah, that's it! I talked to this doc's housekeeper—she said Endermann flew outta there in an awful tear one time. Said he'd never come back and the guy was a quack!"

Doc leaned forward. "What was the doctor's name, Tommy? It may be important."

"Thompson," answered the little man. "Big guy, don' much look like a doc, Doc."

The surgeon sat back, eyes wide. "That explains why he didn't act much like a bodyguard..."

"And, Doc! He's got a big riot planned if he loses the election! Buncha thugs are paid off and waitin' for the signal to cause a buncha trouble in town, bust everythin' up if the big man doesn't come out on top!"

Doc bounced up out of his chair and towards the door. Placing his hand on the doorknob he turned back to his compatriots. "This explains Endermann's need for money and it may even explain his madness room. I think he got more from his psychiatrist than anyone would have imagined. What I can't figure out is why Thompson was in his camp and posing as his bodyguard."

"Where are you going?" Griffin asked.

"I've got a lot to think about," replied Doc soberly. "Much continued luck and good fortune with your manhunt, Captain - I'll be in touch."

Dale Jordan turned her eyes from the cloudy skies above and took in her lunch partners. Though the rain hadn't started up again, there was the promise of more inclement weather in the near future. Fortunately, the little café they occupied was cheerful, in its own quaint way.

"Doesn't Tony look smart today, Dale?" offered Doc Murdock. He waved his fork in the direction of the other man at the table.

Tony Quinn smiled. The handsome man wore dark glasses which covered a series of ugly scars that surrounded his eyes like bracelets. He had been the district attorney of a nearby city who ran afoul of acid thrown by criminals, but now blind contented himself with practicing law and living a bit less harried of a life. He and Doc had been friends for years and had been getting together for lunch as often as their schedules permitted.

"Tony always looks good to me, Miles," said Dale, admiringly.

"Careful now, Dale, or you'll make Doc jealous."

The young nurse blushed and looked sheepishly over at the surgeon. She considered herself quite fortunate to enjoy the company of two such charming men.

"Akelton's in an unprecedented uproar these days," said Quinn. "What's the story, Doc? What's all this about S.J. Endermann reading the riot act to the entire police force?"

Doc set down his fork and wiped the corners of his mouth with his napkin. "I'm afraid I haven't paid much attention to it, Tony. Been too busy with a case. You know how I am about my work."

"I may be blind," the lawyer noted. "But I can sense your tension—and hear the worry in your voice. Is it that tough of a problem for you?"

Dale's face saddened and she looked down at her lap and then out of the corner of her eye at her boss. She couldn't stand to see what he was going through—and that she couldn't tell Tony Quinn the details of the Purple Scar's predicament.

"It's been a tough nut to crack, I must admit," Doc replied seriously. "The patient is something of a celebrity, Tony, and not always available for consultation. Their deformity is one I haven't encountered before, but it runs deep and I'm afraid the entire area around it may be beyond saving. It's not the kind of thing that can just be covered up and forgotten. And there's an element to the case that eludes me at the moment."

"A real mystery, eh?" Quinn stubbed out a cigarette and sat back. "Doc, I've never known anyone who can overcome adversity like you. If anybody can crack this one wide open, its Miles Murdock, the world's greatest plastic surgeon."

His brother's face, his true face, sprung to Doc's mind. Dale's fingers found his hand and gave it a little squeeze.

"Funny, I feel the same way about you, my friend."

"If anybody can crack this one wide open, it's Miles Murdock..."

Quinn lightly touched his dark glasses and smiled. "Well, I guess I've had a tough time or two in the past but the human spirit isn't so easily crushed, I've found. The key is to find something to live for."

"But what if you've, say, lost someone close to you," said Doc. "Very close. A spouse perhaps. Couldn't that just as easily crush you than anything?"

"That's an odd question, coming from you," Quinn retorted. "Take yourself: when John died, how did you get through it? How is it you're sitting with me right now, with this lovely girl at your side?"

Dale blushed again, glad that the lawyer could not see her.

"You could have shut down, called it quits," he continued. "What I'm trying to say is that such adversity can be a two-way street. One could choose a different path than recovery. Horror can twist a man, make him into a monster, an unrecognizable force. You chose to continue John's good works in your clinic and with your patients. That's ultimately commendable in my book."

Doc sat still, soaking in Quinn's words. Something in them wriggled in his brain, begged for attention.

"Some of the world's most terrible dictators might have begun as good men," mused the surgeon. "But power is a heady thing, an electrical force that drives the heart and feeds corruption. I wonder...I wonder..."

Dale grew concerned. "Miles? What is it? You look –"

Doc stood up suddenly, something that had become quite a bad habit for him recently, he thought. Grabbing his hat he placed some bills on top of the meal check and turned to his companions.

"Tony, you've given me much food for thought. I think I might have the solution to my problem—or least the beginnings of one. Thank you!"

He reached for his friend's hand and placed it in his own, shaking it. "Dale can see you to your hotel. I'll...I'll let you know how everything goes."

With that he was gone, leaving Dale and Quinn breathless at his haste.

"Well," said the lawyer. "He acts as if the whole world might be coming to an end!"

+++

Ii had taken him much of the rest of the day to assemble the equipment he needed and to transport it to the required spot. The Purple Scar crouched in the darkness outside of S.J. Endermann's sprawling mansion on the outskirts of Akelton City and waited.

Minutes crawled into hours. He checked his watch every so often. He must be patient, he thought, or everything he'd put together would be for naught. If what he guessed was true, he'd be able to shut the politician down forever.

Voices inside the house drew his attention to the window he huddled beneath. The Scar cranked a small generator to life and lifted a boxy contraption to his eyes.

Luck was with him. Endermann's villainous partner—or was it his master? - conferred with the man once again.

The Purple Scar activated the infra-red apparatus and, looking through it into the darkened room, the answer to the mystery presented itself to him.

The scene at Akelton's largest hotel in the city's teeming downtown was one of excitement and near-pandemonium. An immense crowd had gathered in the square outside the grand old building to listen to their favorite son speak on the eve of his presumed landslide victory.

There was a hum that had spread through the masses, talk of the good things that were surely in store for the state, and of a possible presidential bid in the future. Akelton was aglow with the festivities and all eyes were keen to watch the candidate take the stump.

There had also never been so many policemen and plainclothes officers on the streets at one time.

Doctor Miles Murdock bit his tongue and wound his way through the mob of people. Dale Jordan was right behind him.

Endermann would be almost impossible to get to after he finished speaking. Doc had some small hope that his own credentials and his high standing in the community would see him through to the great man, but he couldn't be sure. The politician would be very well-protected, as no man who had come to the city had ever been guarded before.

Doc kept one ear to what Endermann was saying, high up on the hotel's grand balcony overlooking the square.

"My friends," he said. "In summation, we are a lucky people. We have a will that will see us through any opposition, any weight an enemy can lay upon us. When I look out over this great state of ours, I see hope. An undying measure of hope that gives me pause. I am humbled before it. When I enter our splendid capitol tomorrow, riding on the wave of victory that is sure to come, I will know myself to be blessed by you, the people who believed in me and my campaign. I abjectly thank you."

The crowd went wild. Doc frowned and continued to press on.

Entering the hotel's main lobby, he was greeted by the sight of a throng of reporters and police, all looking a bit pensive and ill-at-ease. The newspapermen had to get a story and the police had to make sure they didn't trample the candidate. It was a stand-off.

Doc and Dale approached a bank of elevators where a band of bluecoats held court. The surgeon affixed a smile to his face and approached a sergeant.

"Hello, Officer," he said pleasantly. "I'm Doctor Miles Murdock. I'd like to see Mr. Endermann for a brief moment, if I may."

"Sure an' everybody would, doctor," announced the surly cop. "I suppose you have something to prove who ya are, hmmm?"

Before Doc could answer, a shadow fell over him and the sergeant. Looking up, Doc saw it was Dan Griffin. The captain wore a funereal look on his face.

"He is who he says he is, Sgt. O'Halloran," Griffin said. "Doctor Miles Murdock, one of our most prominent citizens. I'll vouch for him."

Doc looked squarely at his friend. A long moment passed as the two men stared at each other, neither saying anything. Dale stood between them, glancing at both in turn. She wondered what silent communication passed in that moment.

Finally, Griffin spoke. "Mr. Endermann sees very few people, Doc. Very, very few. He's a busy man. I wouldn't want him bothered by any old thing, you see. It would have to be something pretty important you'd have to say to him."

"Can't think of anything more important than the news I bring him today, Griff. It's practically a matter of life and death."

The captain stretched out a hand and Doc took it. They shook. Dale was sure she had never seen the two men so serious and especially with each other. It scared her.

Doc leaned in a bit to Griffin and spoke softly. "Dan, be ready. Be ready to react. Anything could happen. Trust me."

The captain clapped his friend's arm soundly, turned on his heel and walked away.

✚✚✚

Doc rode up the elevator by himself. Dale had stayed behind at his request. He weighed the odds and there was a possibility that he may not come back down again. No need to bring the lady into it.

While the floor numbers increased Doc took the gum-elastic mask of the Purple Scar out of the deep secret pocket of his coat and spread it out between his hands. His brother's dead face stared back at him. He replaced it in his coat, yet this time in a more swiftly-accessible place.

The lift stopped and the doors opened. Doc was greeted by a coterie of police and a platoon of Endermann's men. He stiffened his spine, took a deep breath and waded in.

One of the officers stopped him. "They called up and told us to expect you, doctor. Mr. Endermann's resting after his speech, but he can spare you a minute or two. Right this way."

They ushered the surgeon into a small side room of a luxurious suite and asked him to wait while they made sure Endermann was ready to receive him. Doc nodded and fingered the mask in his pocket.

A door opened and Eric Boos appeared. "Doctor Murdock? Mr. Endermann will see you now."

The suite beyond was darkened, lit only by a column of light coming in from the half-open doors that led to the balcony. Doc could see the politician was sprawled out in a comfortable chair, one hand stroking his chin and the other holding a glass of something.

Endermann didn't rise. He only looked up at Doc with a tired expression. "Ah, doctor. Please, sit down. What can I do for you?"

"I wonder, Mr. Endermann," Doc began. "If we could talk...privately?"

The candidate narrowed his eyes and frowned slightly. "I've been told you're an upstanding man, doctor, and a pillar of Akelton society. I take it very seriously then that what you have to say is of weight and importance." Endermann looked over at Boos and nodded. "Leave us, Eric. I'll be all right."

The little secretary didn't look so sure but obeyed his boss and exited. The two men were now alone.

"Would you like a drink, Doctor?" said Endermann. He waved in the general direction of the liquor cart.

"No, thank you," answered Doc. "I'll try to be brief. I've recently come across a few items of information that may be of great value to you."

The politician looked questioningly at his guest. "Oh? And what would they be?"

Doc had turned away from Endermann. He took the mask out of his pocket and stretched it over his head. The Purple Scar turned back to his host, with revolver drawn and pointing directly between Endicott's eyes.

"I know your secret," he whispered.

The candidate's eyes widened momentarily. Regaining composure quickly, he simply stared back at the Scar.

"Everyone has secrets," he said flatly. "Mine don't really matter."

The Purple Scar ignored the comment. "You will pay for yours. You will answer to the law. You will not become governor. This thing is over—get up."

Endermann set his drink down and glancing briefly at the door rose from his chair.

"Don't even think about yelling for your boys," hissed the Scar. "I won't hesitate to plug you here and now if I must. And I'm not afraid to die today to make sure you never receive one single vote tomorrow."

Endermann smiled. "You sound very confident, sir. I appreciate that in a man. Listen to that crowd still gathered outside." He gestured to the balcony. "They have confidence in *me*. Do you know what that's worth to a politician?"

"Confidence based on lies and subterfuge," the Purple Scar said. "You never offered any real hope to the people of this state. You've been laughing at them behind their backs the entire time."

The politician said nothing.

"What happened to you after the accident that claimed the life of your dear wife, Mr. Endermann? You didn't have charisma before that, only following it."

"Why, I was shattered by my Molly's death, of course!" objected Endermann. "I had so much hope that she'd be my rock, my touchstone when I attempted to go further with my political career. But she died. And then I sought…help. Help for my mind."

"But you refused treatment!" said the Scar, forcefully.

"Yes," said Endermann. "But only when it became merely words and platitudes. I actually gained something from it, from the chemical side of it. A way of…changing people's minds. Making them see what I saw. Bring them around to my point of view."

The dark avenger stepped back, seemingly angered by the politician's words but his gun never wavering from the target on the man's forehead.

"Hypnotism! Doctor Thompson's preferred treatment for cases of grief—along with a cocktail of chemicals! But, you dispensed with the psychiatrist. Why was he posing then as your bodyguard?"

"Thompson came to me later, after I left his care," whispered Endermann. "Said he could improve upon the treatment, make it better. He begged me to allow him to help my campaign and to offer certain…drugs, should I need a quick pick-me-up now and then. It wouldn't do to have a psychiatrist following me around, so we instituted him as my personal bodyguard. He was certainly a strapping fellow; played the part perfectly."

"Your 'madness room'," the Scar said. "Built around Thompson's own hypnotism experiments and a cracking good idea for political manipulation. Sickening."

Endermann chuckled low in his throat. "Boos and Kowalski relished it even more than I did, the bastards."

"That still doesn't completely explain your meteoric rise to power and influence, Endermann. You were, putting it mildly, a nothing in Akelton. No real gumption or will, only subservience to others. You had to have help, more help than Thompson could offer. You needed a real firebrand, a talker, to get things done. But you didn't have it in you, did you?"

"No, no I didn't, sir," The politician paused, and then spoke again. "I took on a partner. With him, I shall achieve everything I hoped for. Victory is mine."

The Scar tightened his grip on his pistol. "I've heard your 'partner' speak. He's a very worrisome fellow. He'll be the death of you, Endermann."

"When I talk with him, I see the future. He is a true visionary, sir."

"I looked into the room when you were talking with him, Endermann! There was no one else there! *You were talking to yourself!*"

The politician suddenly threw himself to the floor and popped up again just as swiftly. In his hand was a revolver.

The door of the suite flew open and Boos darted into the room, police and goons behind him. The secretary gave a war-cry and started shooting in the general direction of the Purple Scar.

The Scar did not hesitate. Whipping around, he threw himself behind a settee near the balcony and firmly ensconced there returned fire.

The suite quickly filled with gunshots and smoke. The screams of those hit by bullets could be heard and general chaos reigned. The Scar looked around, assessing his position. He spied the doors to the balcony and made a leap towards them.

Gaining the balcony, he quickly flung the doors closed and pulled a heavy metal chaise lounge in front of them, barricading himself from the occupants of the suite.

A clicking noise behind him alerted the Scar to danger. It was Endermann with a gun to the back of his head.

"You're a clever chap," the candidate said. "I might have been able to use someone like you in my stable, but you're a bit unpredictable and that streak of altruism and justice you possess just won't do."

The Purple Scar raised his hands. He took in the situation, examined its facets and observed its possible outcomes. Sounds reached his ears. Sounds of the outdoors, of what seemed like people still gathered in the square but quite possibly a lesser throng then before. And there was also the sound of the men on the other side of the door.

There was also a curious crackling sound.

"Endermann," said the Scar. "Where will you go from here? You'll kill me, of course, but what then? Continue to use me as a symbol to whip up support among the people of Akelton? Parade me through the streets as a trophy of war?"

"You amuse me, my friend. Yes, you've been set up for a pratfall, one that makes me look very, very good, and makes you look very, very bad. Take heart, Purple Scar! You were useful after all!"

"That is good," whispered the Scar. "I'm proud to have served. You in turn must be proud to have served the people."

"Hah!" chortled Endicott. "My other self taught me something: the people are not worthy of my service. They must serve *me!*"

Now it was time for the Scar to laugh. "Excellent, dear sir," he said. "I'm sure they will be glad to hear it."

"Come now, old chap—whatever could you mean?"

"The microphone is still on, and your constituents are still gathered in some force."

Endermann whipped his head back and forth, straining to see if what his adversary said was true. Then, his head blossomed as if a red rose had suddenly supplanted it.

The Purple Scar turned around slowly to see S.J. Endermann lying dead before him from a bullet to the head. Beyond the balcony he could see the faces of a gathering of people, looks of confusion and shock on their faces. They had heard their candidate's words, seen his actions, and they were crushed.

The reign of the politician was over. There would be no victory celebration.

+++

Dan Griffin pushed his hat back on his head and rubbed his forehead. He looked across at his friend, Doctor Miles Murdock and smiled.

"That was a close one," he said.

"Thanks for taking that shot, Dan," said Doc. "That was one in a million."

The two men stood off to one side of the main lobby of the hotel, watching all the hub-bub of the aftermath. Everyone moved with purpose but also with the cold pang of depression hanging over them.

"Forget that," said Griffin. "How did it all fit together?"

The surgeon looked thoughtful and then spoke. "Endermann went a bit crazy after the death of his wife and a kind of second personality manifested in his mind, a much stronger one. What's important to understand is that though he initially sought help, he ultimately refused it when he saw the possibilities in his sickness. His other self was his ticket to the top, or so he thought."

"How did Thompson figure into it?"

"Doctor Thompson was a young psychiatrist with a few ideas for applying hypnotism to cases of schizophrenia. Endermann found his experiments to be crude but ripe with applications—such as convincing others to support his political views. He came very, very close to achieving his goal, Griff. With the governor's seat, he could have used it as a stepping stone to the White House."

The captain shook his head, chagrined. "And he was hiring thugs to rob and pillage? This was to supply him with easy money to feed his gambling and what-not?"

Doc nodded. "Yes, his own efforts at fundraising were so successful that he knew they were being too closely scrutinized. Not a dollar could disappear from his official coffers, so he got criminal elements to scrape up the dirty cash he needed."

Griffin whistled. "Well, what a racket! And on the good will of the people he rode his mighty horse! Makes you kind of wonder about the rest of the lot of speechmakers and babykissers…"

"It's a sad day for Akelton," admitted Doc. "But the power to overcome adversity, to see one's self through a tough time is one of the incredible strengths of mankind. Endermann's star will continue to fall until it's forgotten, hopefully forever. The man was a coward—he ran out from the attack he orchestrated on his own fundraiser because he couldn't stand to witness any violence firsthand. His other self allowed him free rein for his deep-rooted anger and it manifested itself in a voice that directed crime… and murder. And, curiously, both halves of his warped mind seem to come together there at the end, when he held the gun on me."

He stopped there and pondered a thought.

"When Endermann decreed that the Purple Scar be brought in, in some ways I see it as his own self-loathing rising to the top, recognition of his own inability to bring justice to the world."

Griffin looked at his friend, a sympathetic look come over his face.

"Sorry about the manhunt, Doc. The good thing is that the Purple Scar is no longer a wanted man—well, at least for the moment." He smiled warmly at the joke.

Lightly punching Doc in the arm, the captain suddenly flung up his arms. "Hey, I've got it! The answer to the Scar's popularity problem! Maybe *he* should run for public office!"

The look on Doc's face spoke volumes and Griffin quieted down.

"Not on your life, my friend. Not on your life!"

THE END

THE PURPLE SCAR. WHAT A NAME!

Stop me if you've heard this one before...

Having approached Ron Fortier about writing pulp for Airship 27, he had me "audition" by crafting a 2-page sample that would, hopefully, prove my pulp suitability. Gleeful, I wrote a Doc Savage scene and loaded it with everything about pulp—and Doc—that I love. Thankfully, Lester Dent looked down upon me favorably and passing Prof. Ron's scrutiny he provided me with a list of potential pulp protagonists from which I should pick a path. After a bit of haggling—how could one pick?—Ron suggested I put my pulp-laden pen to paper and proselytize over the Purple Scar.

I first came across the character in the pages of Don Hutchison's *The Great Pulp Heroes*, and though the Scar was buried in a chapter along with other almost-rans I jotted him down on a list of pulp stars I hoped to read more about one day. What can I say? I'm a list-maker. Flash forward to last year: I was offered the chance to not read about him but to *write* about him. Ordering a copy of Altus Press' Purple Scar collection, I then hunkered down to the reading part.

Hutchison calls Miles Murdock a "hero with distinct, although somewhat unrealized possibilities," who possessed a masked identity that was "utterly bizarre." What more could a writer ask for? Potential... possibility...pure pulp pandemonium. Yep, that's for me. This was a character that had a total of four stories in his official files but, I felt, who surely had more to tell us.

Emboldened by Ron's faith in me and hoping that the great pulp scribes were still looking over my shoulder, I set out to accomplish three objectives with my Purple Scar tale: to turn up the violence, provide a higher-class of villain and to utilize the physical nature of the Scar's horrifying visage to more dramatic effect. Oh, and to tell a good story. Wait, that's four, isn't it?

Although the violence isn't exactly of Norvell Page caliber, I wanted Doc Murdock to be a bit more *straightforward* when dispatching criminals in "Satan on the Stump." He wasn't any shrinking violet back in 1941, of course, but I wanted him to be able to look The Shadow and The Spider in the eye as an equal should he ever have run into them. So, Doc shoots things a lot more.

Funny thing about my villain: I can't remember how I tumbled onto the idea of placing him in the political arena, save that it would make for a theme not often played out in pulp literature. I'm not a very political person myself, which is why our baddie's party is never revealed—but it will be interesting to hear your thoughts on the matter. Above and beyond that, I simply thought that the Purple Scar deserved better than the rather tepid thugs and other uninspiring problems he'd faced in the past.

As for the face of the Purple Scar, well, that's the key to the whole shebang, right? There had to be much, much more going on with a guy who wore the face of his murdered brother's corpse and the sight he'd have presented to his opponents. I don't know about you, but if I ran into a gun-toting mook with a face that looked like he'd been soaking underwater after having been brutally killed I think that's an image that'd stick with me for a long, long time. In fact, I believe he might have actually caused a few hearts to stop...

I can't tell you how much I enjoyed writing "Satan on the Stump" and playing around in the weird world of the Purple Scar. I hope you dig the story and please let me know if you did. You can also tell me if you hated it, too—a writer cannot live on praise alone!

By the way, the tale originally had chapter titles but I handed it in right as the edict came down to dispense with such in these shorter stories. For all you completists out there, here are the original titles, in order: "Party Crashers," "Manhunt," "The Right Honorable Mr. Endermann," "The Madness Room," "Starved for Information" and "Poll Results."

And one last little bit of trivia: right up until the very last moment before I delivered the story, my villain's last name was "Endicott"...but I thought that was a bit too much.

+++

JIM BEARD - a native of Toledo, Ohio, was introduced at an early age to the great pulp characters by his father, who himself had thrilled to the adventures of The Shadow, Zorro and The Green Hornet as a child. As a young adult and inspired by an interview with pulp scribe Will Murray, Jim picked up his first Doc Savage paperback and was soon engulfed in the Man of Bronze's tales. A pulp fan was born.

After decades of reading, collecting and dissecting comic books, Jim became a published writer when he sold a story to DC Comics in 2002. Since that time he's written Star Wars and Ghostbusters comic stories and contributed articles and essays to several volumes of comic book history. He is also the editor of *Gotham City 14 Miles*, a book of essays on the 1960s *Batman* TV series.

Currently, Jim provides regular content for Marvel.com, the official Marvel Comics website, is a regular columnist for Toledo Free Press and is also writing a book about the comics industry during the decade that made him the huge fan he is today, the 1970s.

THE PURPLE SCAR'S REVENGE
BY JONATHAN FISHER

Doctor Miles Murdock, M.D., stood silently in what remained of the lobby of his lower slums clinic. Half a dozen bodies lay scattered, charred, and disfigured around him. Three were easily identifiable by size as men. Their weapons identified them further. The charred remains of a violin case, a scorched Thompson submachine-gun inside. Pearl-handled pistols, some semi-automatic, one other revolver.

The other three were going to be harder to identify. Their bodies were destroyed in the explosion that had burned the clinic to the ground. The oxygen storage tanks had ruptured in the fight, and that sparked a ferocious fire that trapped three Mafioso's inside with three innocents.

Captain Dan Griffin of Akelton homicide approached, took a long drag on his cigarette, and tossed it into the smoldering embers of a nearby timber.

"What a gawd-awful mess."

"Yeah," Murdock sighed, "do you have any suspects?"

"No," Griffin said, "but these guys belonged to Donahue's gang."

"How do you figure?"

"Their guns. Donahue's top level enforcers favor those pearl-gripped pieces. Thinks it makes 'em a special kind of fancy."

"No doubt," Murdock said, "Do you have any other leads?"

"Not in here,' he said. "Outside, maybe so."

Murdock followed the elder cop out into the street. Evidence markers littered the area.

"Walk me through it then, Dan," Murdock said.

"A black Ford sedan comes to a stop, here," he gestures to a set of skid marks on the pavement, "three shooters get out, fan across the street. They open up, and start shredding the place."

Three separate evidence markers denoted the piles of spent brass casings that littered the ground in the center of the street, and next to two parked cars.

"Were there any shots returned from inside?"

"Not a one," Griffin said.

"Who were these guys?"

"My best guess is that they were O'Hara's thugs. Donahue's been doing business on O'Hara's land for a while now. Maybe O'Hara got sick of it."

"That'd make sense, but why attack the clinic?"

"Maybe O'Hara's goons followed Donahue's here, and ambushed them."

"And blew up my clinic," Murdock sighed.

"Yeah, Doc, they did do that."

Miles Murdock looked around slowly, made sure no one else was in ear shot and said, "You do understand that I have to deal with this now."

"Yeah, I do. Just don't make mess of my city."

"I can't make promises like that, Dan, and you know it."

"Yeah, well, try. For me."

"Fine," Murdock said, and walked away towards his Buick Straight-8. It was brand new, a powerful machine with elegance and class. He would be very surprised if it weren't stolen by the end of the evening. Before he got busy with the night's events, however, he stopped at his mansion up on Swank Street, and collected a few things.

✝✝✝

Shale's Jazz Emporium sat on the corner of 23rd and Belmont, just north of Broadway. It had aluminum walls, and a blue neon sign labeled the place. Just inside the double doors, two bodyguards stood, out of sight. Around the back, down the alley was a single iron door with a smaller, red neon sign that said, Paisley's Gym. It was where all of Douglas O'Hara's boxers trained, and where the bookies brought information about who was an up-and-comer, and how to fix the fights.

Miles Murdock, M.D., walked down the alley towards the back door. He pulled the door open, stepped through. Bad cigar smoke, the smell of sweat and blood mixed with saw-dust all wafted up to Murdock. He took a deep breath, then pushed through the inner door. He was met at the bottom by a hulking tough-guy with a badly fitted suit and an ugly fedora.

"Hold up there," he said, then frisked Murdock. When he was finished, he asked "Whaddya want?"

"I want to talk to O'Hara."

"The boss ain't in right now."

"It's urgent. Unless you'd rather I took this matter to the police."

The tough hesitated, then said, "Wait here," and went over to the phone. Murdock looked around. A ring was in the center of the room with stained canvas and gauze on the edges of the ropes keeping them intact. Two men were inside the ring, one big guy, with shoulders that looked like they were carved out of granite, and a smaller guy wearing padding and dancing around.

"Use your left!" the coach kept yelling. "Hook him with your left!"

The coach was a pot-bellied old man with a balding head and a mean face. He was chewing on a cigar.

"Come on," the tough guy said, and led Murdock back past the ring. The office in back was broad, with thick glass, a heavy door. Inside was a wide desk, a large humidor on the surface, and an older gentleman wearing a dark gray pinstripe suit behind the desk.

The tough stepped aside, and Murdock pushed through the door. O'Hara didn't rise.

"You need somethin' else?" he said to the guy across from his desk, "You've got your instructions."

The man nodded, rose, and left. He was tall, athletically built, but when he passed Murdock, the Doctor caught a distinct scent of something decaying. It was very distinctive, almost like putrefaction.

"Good evening, Mr. Murdock," O'Hara said, and tipped his cigar towards the Doctor.

"*Doctor* Murdock, actually."

"Oh yes," O'Hara smiled, "You operate that clinic down in, uh, south Akelton."

"That's a nice way to describe it. And yes, I *did* operate a clinic. I used to, anyway, until about eleven o'clock tonight."

"I'm sorry to hear that. What happened?"

"We're intelligent men, Mr. O'Hara. Don't act like you don't know."

"Anything you ask me to confess to right now is entrapment."

"I don't want to go to the police," Murdock said, "I want to know why you thought it'd be a good idea to ambush opposing forces in my clinic."

"I've been accused of a lot of things, but never of attacking someone in a hospital," he laughed, and looked up at his body-guard. "Make a note of that. I'll have to try it some time."

"Yes, sir," the tough guy said.

"I'm not laughing. Why are you?"

"Doc, you've got stones, I'll give you that. I'm a businessman, and I run a good deal of it. See, it'd be bad for me, my reputation, and my public image if I attacked a hospital. So why would you think I'd do such a thing?"

"Because those were Lawrence Donahue's men that were ambushed, and everyone with half a brain knows that you and Donahue aren't getting along real well right now."

"That is very true," O'Hara said, "but you've only accounted for two thirds of the criminal equation of Akelton. What about Giovanni Rebisi's crew? Everyone knows how easily he takes offense and how happy he is to draw blood over any infraction of honor that he sees."

"Are you going to honestly tell me you had nothing to do with my clinic being blown up?"

"I am going to honestly say so."

"Then there's just one other thing, technically, if I cared about such things: my clinic operated in your turf, did it not?"

"It did indeed, Doctor Murdock." He took a long drag on his cigar, he acted carefree, but Murdock could see in the mob boss's eyes that he was getting wary.

"Would protecting it fall under your jurisdiction?"

Murdock smiled inwardly as he watched O'Hara's eyes narrow.

"What are you getting at?"

"Shouldn't finding out who destroyed the clinic be a concern of yours? For the well-being of the citizens under your protection, of course, and your public image."

O'Hara stamped out the cigar and studied Murdock carefully. Murdock said nothing, did not smile, kept his face utterly neutral. He had no doubt that he was intellectually smarter than O'Hara. The tricky part of this little plan was getting O'Hara into a place where his sense of honor would cause him to act rashly.

"I'd say that it might. If you cared about such things, but you've just told me that you don't."

"Because none of your business affected mine. But now that it does, the status quo needs to be readdressed."

"What did you have in mind?"

"I want to know who attacked my clinic, and I want restitution paid."

"If you really want to know, ask Rebisi. He always spills some blood before he makes a land-grab. It's his trademark," O'Hara sneered.

"Thank you," Murdock said, and rose slowly.

"Doctor Murdock?"

Miles turned.

"Walk away from this. If it is Rebisi, it will be taken care of."

Murdock nodded, then walked away. He smiled as he got to the door, walked into the alley. Now he just needed to wait, and follow the car that O'Hara would inevitably dispatch to 'deal' with this new problem.

+++

It didn't take much effort to follow O'Hara's crew. They made no efforts to evade a tail, even if they'd been aware of Murdock's presence in the Straight-8. They cruised west, towards the river, and the warehouse district. Rebisi controlled most of the shipping in and out of Akelton. Even his legitimate front corporations consisted of import-export firms.

Two fences divided Rebisi's compound. The outer storage yard had a massive front entrance with smooth curb to drive over. The inner yard was guarded with a taller fence, a single gate in or out, with a large transport truck kept off to one side.

Murdock fell back to a half mile's distance as the O'Hara car cruised into the compound. Doc Murdock drove over the curb, and stopped behind some shipping pallets, and climbed out. He took a .38, his police badge, a set of master-keys, and put on his mask.

Several years ago, his brother, an honest cop, was murdered, his face burned with acid, and dumped in the river. He'd been submerged for ten days, and by the time he was recovered, that destroyed face was so hideous that anyone who looked on it went slightly mad with horror and revulsion. When Miles had been called to identify his brother, he'd taken the look of his brother's face personally, copied it exactly as a mask, and wore it to fight the crime of Akelton as the gruesome avenger known as the Purple Scar.

He closed the driver's door to the Buick, kept the revolver in hand, and started across the storage yard towards the second fence where the central warehouse for all of Rebisi's 'enterprises.'

In the shadows between a row of storage pallets, the Scar checked to make sure the mask was snug against his skin. It was thin and flexible, and with the coloring of the scar-tissue, the mask obscured his face in the shadows, made him mostly invisible.

He stopped near the fence. It's made of chain link, nine feet tall, with one gate. The three O'Hara cars pulled to a stop at the gate, hesitated. While they sat there, men poured out of the warehouse to greet the convoy. Finally, the car was let through. Guns were drawn on the O'Hara crew.

The Purple Scar jogged towards a dark patch of fence, leapt at it, climbed over, and dropped into darkness.

The O'Hara dispatch came to a stop, and six men piled out. They were frisked and disarmed by the Rebisi gang, and led inside. All of Rebisi's more illegal wares were kept behind the second fence, in secret storage areas of the warehouse.

The Purple Scar kept to the darkness, slinked around towards the warehouse itself. Several guards remained outside, wary of an ambush. He swung wide around them, going for a back door. He was halfway there, scuttled along a row of containers when he heard a man sigh and the flick of a lighter.

He hesitated. A man stepped into view, leaned against the container the Scar was hidden next to. He had a cigarette in his mouth. He looked at the fence. If this guy turned his head to the left at all, the Scar would be spotted.

Silently, making each step slowly, easing his weight onto the lead foot only after he was sure nothing would betray him, the Scar crept up on the guard. The man smoked slowly. The Purple Scar got closer, six feet, then four.

The man turned to the left, flicked his cigarette out into an empty part of the yard, he spotted the horrifying Purple Scar. He stood up straight and opened his mouth to yell.

The grim masked avenger lunged forward, smashed his hand into the throat, paralyzed the vocal chords. The man staggered, and the Scar grabbed him by his tie. He dragged him forward, punched him in the kidney, then twisted the goon around. He kicked the back of the knee, and the man dropped. The Purple Scar grabbed the man's jaw, and twisted hard. There was a pop, and the man slumped to the ground.

The Scar dragged him to the deepest shadows next to the container, then kept moving towards the back door of the warehouse.

A single guard stood directly under the light that hung in front of the door. He had a fedora on his head, and a pistol in his hand. Further along the wall, at the corner, another guard stood.

Back door's out, the frightening vigilante realized. He looked around rapidly, searching for a way.

There were several stacks of tarp-covered boxes made of wood along the wall to the right of the back-door guard. Above these was an open window, folded out about two feet. The Purple Scar smiled. It would almost be too easy.

He kept to a low crouch, moved around the edges of the pallets and containers, trying to keep out of the guard's sightlines. He avoided being back-lit; that'd be almost as bad as walking directly under one of the lights in the compound.

Doc Murdock hesitated at the edge of the pallets. He was close enough that most sounds would carry to the guard. He had to chance it; there was no way to approach the guard, and drag him out of the back-door's light without being spotted and nominated for sainthood.

Slowly, carefully, the masked man eased his weight up onto the pallets. He was grateful that the containers seemed stable, at least. He took a slow step forward. He made no noise on the slick tarpaulin. He reached up grasped the edge of the window, then bent his knees. He sprang upward, hooked a leg over the seam. His shoe brushed the edge of the sheet metal. The guard turned.

The Scar dropped inside before he was spotted. His shoes clicked quietly when he landed.

"What's up?" a voice asked.

"I thought I saw somethin'."

The Purple Scar slinked forward, kept his gun in hand, moved through the deep shadows at the walls of the warehouse. He got to the farthest corner from the back door when it creaked open. A guard came through with a flashlight. He shone the light on the window, then down around the spot where the avenger had landed.

"See anything?" the first voice asked.

"Nah," the second said, looked for a moment longer, then moved back through the door, and left the warehouse in darkness.

The Purple Scar let out a pent-up breath, and looked around. The warehouse was divided into sections. A catwalk network ran near the roof. The walks passed through the individual sections without doors. Lights hung down from the ceiling, below the walks. It was the natural place to spot the meeting from.

There was a ladder on the other side of this section, and a guard standing near it. He stood at the edge of the light, his eyes hidden from view. Deep shadow flanked the walls, but several lights hung near the ladder. A stealth approach, where the Purple Scar went up the ladder without alerting the guard, was out of the question.

From what he could see, the guard's back was against the wall. The Scar swore softly to himself. It could never be simple.

He kept low, moved around the walls, made his way towards the guard. His shoe scuffed on the floor while he watched the guard. The head moved, and the Scar froze. He lifted his pistol very slowly. He didn't want to have to shoot; that would screw up his entire plan.

The guard stared for a long moment, then looked away. After a moment's hesitation, he looked down at something he was worrying in his hands.

The Purple Scar kept moving.

Finally, he was on the same wall as the guard. Almost on his hands and knees, he slid up towards the guard. The warehouse was deathly still, no noise other than the guard's rhythmic breathing filled the void. The Purple Scar's own respiration was shallow, silent.

Ten feet now. Eight. Three more steps, and bizarre crimefighter could grab him, probably snap his neck before he was aware. The Scar looked down, realized the object the guard was fiddling with in his hands was a knife.

The guard lunged, stabbed straight at the Purple Scar. He recoiled, staggered backwards. The guard hacked in again, slashed at him, then stabbed straight at his chest.

How did he see me?

The guard tore his fedora off, his eyes open wide. It was the look of a crazed man, out for blood.

The Purple Scar growled. Two could play at this game.

The man slashed again. The Scar lunged, blocked the stab, then drove his knee up into the man's gut. He shoved the goon backwards into the light. The Scar chased after him.

When the harsh light fell across the mask of the Purple Scar, the guard's eyes went wide, not with crazed rage, but with terror. The man stared at the ruined face. Nothing he had ever looked upon was so terrible. It was the face of a rotted corpse. It was something hell itself had created, only to spit it back out in revulsion.

The horror lunged forward, wrenched the blade out of the paralyzed hand of the guard, and held it up to the man's throat.

"Is there a good reason I shouldn't kill you?" the Purple Scar snarled.

"I-I-I can help," He stuttered.

"How?"

"I know some stuff."

"Start talking."

"I know da boss is makin' a land-grab, picking up pieces of Donahue's and O'Hara's territory while the other two are squarin' off against each odder."

"Why?"

"Because O'Hara doesn't take da Boss's threats seriously. Rebisi's got Akelton by the throat. He's gonna prove it, too."

"How?"

"I don't know how," the guard whimpered, tried to avert his eyes from the horror that the mask was. The Purple Scar shifted, made the guard look.

"Open your eyes or I'll cut them open," the Scar growled.

The man opened his eyes slowly. He went weak at the knees, started stuttering, and couldn't make a coherent thought.

The Purple Scar caught a whiff of something foul suddenly. He looked down. The guard's charcoal gray suit was darker around the crotch. The Scar punched him in the throat, then shoved him backwards. The man staggered to the ground, held onto his ruined throat.

"Stay silent, don't get brave, and you'll keep breathing."

The man nodded slowly. The masked vigilante headed for the ladder. A moment later, the guard passed out.

The catwalk was dusty. The Purple Scar was careful as he moved along, keeping silent and unobtrusive. He had no intentions of being caught today, not after what it took to get in here.

"I have no incentive to talk to you," he heard a strong Italian-accented voice said.

"Our Boss is willing to let you continue to live and work in this city," this from one of O'Hara's thugs.

"He's going to let me…" Rebisi shrieked with laughter. "How gracious of him."

"You should listen to what we have to offer. A war between our families is bad for business on both sides," O'Hara's emissary said.

"What if war is my business?"

"Then I'd say we have nothing more to discuss."

The O'Hara clan stood slowly.

"You're making a big mistake," Rebisi said

The Purple Scar moved closer to see better.

"The mistake is in on your end, not ours," O'Hara's emissary said. He turned, and walked towards the front door. Rebisi said something quickly in Italian, and gunfire erupted from the far sides of the room. Men from O'Hara's troupe fell rapidly as the gunfire cut inward. The leader dropped flat as others fell dead. Blood spread rapidly, dark pools of it all over.

The Purple Scar pulled his pistol, aimed down at the gunmen below him. The gunfire ceased suddenly.

The emissary was flat on the floor, but he crawled forward. He looked unwounded.

"Tell O'Hara what happened. Tell him this is a prelude to what will befall his family if he should persist." Rebisi waved his hands, and two men rushed forward, grabbed the emissary, and hauled him to his feet.

The Scar took another step. Something creaked beneath him, bolts popped, and metal shrieked as it was rent. The catwalk tumbled down. He threw himself off it as it crumbled. He crashed to the floor amid a cloud of dust and debris. He shoved to his feet in the midst of the shock, and grabbed the closest gunman.

"Kill him!" Rebisi screamed, pointed at the Purple Scar. The two men dragged the emissary out of the building.

The Scar pressed his pistol against the man's head. The human shield whimpered as the grim avenger dragged him backwards. Rebisi's gunmen hesitated, unwilling to kill their friend.

"I said shoot him now!" the Italian boss screamed.

When no one did, he pulled out his own revolver, and fired one shot into the Scar's human shield. The bullet tore into the man's chest. He gasped, then went limp.

"Crap," the Purple Scar hissed.

The man became dead weight. The Scar couldn't hold him upright. He dragged him backwards, trying to keep the body between him and the shooters now lined up against him. Most carried long rifles with huge drum magazines. Thompsons, by the looks of things.

The door behind him opened suddenly. The Purple Scar stared, the man he'd knocked out was upright, a cut in his scalp bleeding profusely. The Scar shoved the body away from him, and lunged at the other man.

Gunfire roared as a simultaneous wall of thunder. The Scar threw himself behind the man, and into the other side of the warehouse. He sprinted hard towards the back door.

It opened suddenly. The Purple Scar snapped his pistol up, fired one shot, missed, a second shot, and that one winged the man that came through the door. A third shot fired, into the man's chest. The fourth put him down.

The Purple Scar slowed, stooped, grabbed the man's pistol, and kept running. The gunmen were fanning out into the stock yard now, firing blindly at the shadows.

One guard, close at hand, fired a burst at the Scar, and suddenly all fire shifted towards him. The Purple Scar fired twice from his revolver, then fired twice more from the .45 automatic he'd picked up off the dead goon.

He kept running. He tore into the darkness near the inner fence, and slowed quickly. Fast movement would give him away now.

He crept along the pallets and containers, keeping low and silent. The gunmen moved in all around him. He could hear them. His heart hammered brutally against the wall of his ribs. He held his breath, scarcely able to breathe.

Footsteps clapped against the pavement near him. He hesitated, stole

"Kill him!" Rebisi screamed…"

a glance around the corner. A single gunman with a Thompson was approaching slowly. The Purple Scar swore bitterly in the silence of his mind. This man was thorough, professional. He approached each corner slowly, panned his sights around the edges to make sure he wouldn't be jumped, then moved forward.

He was good.

Behind him, the Purple Scar heard another man. He turned, saw a tall goon with a shotgun to his shoulder. The Scar crouched, then leapt straight up. His hands seized on the edge of the container, and he hauled himself onto the top. He looked back. The man with the shotgun walked away.

The gunman with the Thompson was at the Scar's container. The rest of the goons had moved over to the front gate, while only a scarce half dozen were searching through the storage yard. They began climbing into the truck parked near the gate.

The Purple Scar slid to the edge, peered down on the man. He swept around the right corner slowly, then ducked across the gap between containers, and swept around the left. The Scar dropped straight down on the gunsel, shoved the gun to the side and punched the man in the throat. The big fellow gagged, tried to back up, bring his rifle to bear. The Scar drove a knee brutally up into the man's groin, then wrenched him forward.

The Thompson dropped to the pavement. The Scar spun the gunman around, kicked his knee out from under him, then snapped his neck. The Purple Scar picked up the Thompson, then moved closer to the fence. The man with the shotgun was just out of sight now. He climbed the fence slowly, as quietly as he could.

A shot rang out behind him.

"There he is!"

The grisly avenger threw himself bodily over the fence, landed awkwardly on the pavement. He yelled in agony as he landed on his shoulder, which bore the full weight of him. He staggered to his feet, and raced past the pallets towards his parked car.

A solid wall of gunfire roared behind him. He ducked in behind a pallet, which was instantly besieged. Lead tore into it, shredded it, sent small puffs of dust and splinters into the air.

Using the Thompson, the Purple Scar fired a burst blindly around the corner of the pallet. Gunfire broke off for a moment. He twisted then braced himself. He slammed his dislocated shoulder into the hard wood of the crates, and screamed in pain.

"Kill him!" Rebisi screamed.

The Purple Scar fired, then rushed from behind his pallet towards the next one, closer to his car. Gunfire stopped for a moment, and the Scar broke into a dead-sprint, straight towards the Buick. The Thompson clicked empty, and he dropped it. He slid in next to the driver's door, wrenched it open, and dropped behind the wheel. He twisted the key, and dropped it into gear.

He angled towards the perimeter, saw the fence, spun the wheel left. He slid sideways, almost lost it, held the slide, and got straightened out. He buried his foot in it, tore past the metal fence. He was almost clear.

A horn blared suddenly from the right, he looked, saw the huge delivery truck coming out of Rebisi's yard. The Purple Scar steered right, pushed his foot harder into the floor. The car tore into the metal fencing, when the truck hit him in the back left.

The Buick spun around. The Purple Scar tried to steer out of it, but he couldn't. He spun into a metal pole, crashed on the driver's side, rebounded, and came to a stop in the middle of the street.

His mind was dazed, fogged by the impact and the gunfight.

He tried the key, the engine ticked, stuttered, almost caught, but didn't.

"Take him inside, boys," a voice yelled.

The Purple Scar lifted his pistol. He saw one gunman come into view, fired a shot. The bullet went wide, the man ducked, but he kept coming.

The gun clicked empty. He searched for spare shells, found none. His shoulder ached painfully as he moved.

The door was torn open, rough hands dragged him out. He landed on the pavement, and a man screamed. The avenger realized the mask was still on, and for a moment, he had hope that it would keep them from discovering his true identity.

A punch landed brutally on his face. He gagged on the hit, but could not move.

"Get him inside," Rebisi said, much more quietly now, much closer.

In the distance, a siren wailed, then two, then too many to make out individual sirens. The Purple Scar smiled.

"Let me go, or all of them come in to talk to you."

"The cops want you dead as badly as the rest of us."

"Not quite. They back me up."

The hands that had been carrying him dropped him. He moaned, his body went rigid with agony.

"Take his guns, get inside," Rebisi snarled.

He was frisked painfully, everything of value was taken from him, including the police badge he carried, just in case. It was handed up to Rebisi, who swore bitterly.

"Keep my business to yourself, or the only business you'll ever do is from six feet underground." Cop or no, killing anyone with a badge meant the cops would come down on him like a ton of bricks.

The gunman departed quickly as the sirens got closer. The Purple Scar turned slowly, watched Rebisi's goons depart. When they were out of sight, he reached up, and took off his mask slowly. He slid it into the secret pocket of his coat, and dragged himself towards his car.

The cops came rolling up in force, but none of them approached the compound. Captain Dan Griffin got out of a Ford Sedan, spotted Dr. Miles Murdock and jogged over to him.

"What happened?"

"I'll tell you when we're clear."

Griffin helped Murdock back to his sedan.

"How will you proceed here?" Murdock asked.

"I won't. We're getting out of here. I heard about a body being dragged out of here, so I came to investigate, got caught up in all this ruckus."

"Will they go in?"

"Probably not," Griffin said. "Not enough numbers to handle what's inside. Everyone knows Rebisi would love to square with anyone who dares to challenge him. We won't give him the excuse."

"Then let's go."

"Right."

Doc Murdock slumped in his seat, and Griffin drove away.

The coffee was stale, the breakfast plate was mostly cold, but nevertheless, Murdock ate gratefully. Captain Griffin sat across from him, a cup of coffee in his hands.

"Any particular reason you decided to drop in there?"

"After I talked, face to face, with O'Hara, I figured that he'd send some guys over to Rebisi's joint to rustle his feathers. Seems I was right."

"What did that accomplish?"

"I don't think Rebisi is behind the killings at my clinic."

"You do realize that this isn't the first gunfight that's happened recently?"

"Yeah. This is what, the fifth or sixth gang-related shoot-out in the past month?"

"Sixth, almost seventh if Rebisi had been allowed to finish on you.

The three families are ready to declare war. There aren't enough cops in Akelton to keep it from being burnt down."

"So who stands to gain the most?"

"I have no idea," Captain Griffin said. "Organized crime isn't my purview insofar as the business of it is concerned."

"It's only when the bodies start dropping that things fall into your purview?"

"Don't pin this on me," Griffin snapped. "I've been very understanding about your vendetta, something I've been kind enough to keep to my own self."

"I didn't say you weren't. I'm just saying you're not helping me stop this war before it gets out of hand."

"What do you think I'm doing? I'm not just organizing all the crooked cops into a nice, neat row to keep them out of trouble."

"Just stop talking, Dan."

"No, you listen to me good and hard, Murdock, because when I tell you I'm doing my damndest to clean this mess up, you better believe me."

"Fine. Tell me where Donahue has his headquarters, for a start."

"Why do you want to corner him?"

"He's the only gang that I've heard of that hasn't been affected as brutally as Rebisi or O'Hara."

"He has an office building uptown. It's a nice place, but well defended. It's going to be nearly impossible to get into."

"Let me worry about that."

Griffin continued to sip at his coffee. Miles Murdock massaged his shoulder. He looked absently out the window. Several cars drove by, none of which looked too exciting. When a lone black sedan slowed, looked at the police cruiser that Captain Griffin drove, it turned around at the intersection, a bad presentiment came over him.

"Hey, Dan," Murdock started.

The suicide doors on the sedan swung open, and two men leaned out. Doc lunged across the table, grabbed Captain Griffin by the collar, and dragged him out of the booth. Murdock's own gun was missing; he took Griffin's as they hit the floor.

"Everybody down!"

The machine-gunners opened up on the diner, peppered the windows, blowing them inward. Lights went out, jars exploded, sparks flew everywhere. The waitress was too stunned to move, and bullets stitched across her chest. She slumped behind the counter.

Most customers got down. Murdock crawled rapidly towards the hallway behind his booth, where a back door was. When he was out of sight of the sedan driving by, he threw himself upright, and burst through the back door.

The sedan accelerated, the engine roared. Murdock fired at the car, peppered the back until the cylinder was empty. The back window shattered, one man was thrown forward and a mist of red erupted inside. Then it weaved out of sight, around the corner.

Murdock emptied the spent casings, ran back inside.

Captain Griffin climbed to his feet. He looked around. Murdock handed back the cop's pistol.

"Whatever you need," Captain Griffin said, "you've got it."

"I need a bigger gun," Murdock decided.

✝✝✝

The building was six stories. The first five floors held offices, accounting firms all owned and operated by Lawrence Donahue. The top floor was a penthouse, a lavish series of suites all owned and lived in by William Donahue, third generation Irish mobster.

Murdock sat in Griffin's battered sedan, looked at the building. No guards were visible, they'd all be inside. But the back door was in the alley, and that would be guarded openly by Donahue thugs.

"How do you think you can play it?"

"The building on the right."

Next to Donahue's headquarters was a sturdy, but much older building that looked relatively disused. The rooftops were level with each other, and the gap between buildings didn't look that daunting.

"Keep rolling," Murdock said. "If I'm not out in an hour, or if you don't hear from me by two A.M., send help."

"I got it," Captain Griffin said. Back at the diner, Murdock had helped himself to the reserve weapons in the trunk of Dan Griffin's car. Murdock climbed out. He had a .38 in his shoulder rig, but he also had a .45 at the small of his back with a pocket-full of clips. He was ready to make good on the little piece of war that had been thrust upon him.

The back door of the building next to Donahue's was locked, but after two hits with his good shoulder, it heaved, and he helped himself inside. The shoulder he'd dislocated at Rebisi's storage yard ached, his back hurt, his head felt like it was slowly and methodically being removed from his shoulders. It wasn't the worst shape he'd ever been in to go to war, he reflected.

The building seemed abandoned, but he took his time as he climbed to the top floor. The door to the roof was jammed, and he couldn't budge it with his shoulder. He kicked it furiously, and on the fifth volley, it creaked, and swung open. Someone had braced it closed from the outside.

Murdock saw no guards on either rooftop. He jogged to the edge, and measured the gap. Eight feet, give or take.

"I can make that," he decided.

He jogged half way across the roof, hesitated, pulled his fedora on tight, took two fast breaths, then fell into a sprint. He raced forward, and leapt.

He cleared the distance easily, landed on the balls of his feet, tucked and rolled. He slid to a stop in a crouch, and groaned. His shoulder ached more profusely than before. He stood, headed for the roof door that led down to the penthouse level of the Donahue office building.

Four feet from the door, it swung outward, and a goon in a cheap black suit stepped out. He had a cigarette in his mouth, puffed on it absently.

Murdock braced coiled to attack.

"I know why I'm here," the goon said. "Why are you?"

Murdock found himself saying, "Don't you need fresh air once in a while too?"

The man nodded, then stepped aside. Murdock stared incredulously at the man as he walked off to the middle of the roof to smoke absently. Murdock stepped through the door, and pulled the mask of the Purple Scar out of the secret pocket of his coat. He removed his hat, donned the mask and then pulled his fedora back on snuggly.

Now it was time to get mean.

He descended the narrow stairs slowly, found the door at the bottom open. He peered around the door jamb. Two guards stood in front of a broad set of double-doors, beyond which the Purple Scar assumed the penthouse was kept.

The Scar heard dishes clank together, something being shifted. He looked around and saw a broad swinging door that led into what looked like a private kitchen.

The shadows were deep at the end of the hall. The two guards at the door looked tired, mostly oblivious. One was seated, reading a paperback, the other was talking on the telephone set on a table across the hallway.

The Purple Scar put his back to the wall, slid slowly along it towards the kitchen door. There was a single round porthole that looked inside. The kitchen itself was well lighted, with one man working inside it. There was a silver tray laid out, several pieces of food on it. A push-cart was next to the end of the central cooking island. Grills and stoves were against the farthest wall, while several tall metal-framed shelves held every imaginable cooking utensil.

The chef walked away from the platter he fussed over, and filled a silver bucket with ice. The Scar spotted a heavy-looking ladle next to the saucepan the chef had been working by, grabbed it, and lunged at the chef. He bashed the man hard down on the back of the skull. The man pitched forward. The Purple Scar grabbed him by his collar, lowered him to the ground and headed for the door.

There was a single door between the kitchen and the penthouse suites. The Purple Scar took a deep breath, and peered through the swinging door into the penthouse. It had a porthole, just like the one into the kitchen from the outside hallway.

The room was vast, with three love seats spread out around the fire, bookshelves on each wall, and a giant phonograph with a cabinet full of vinyl records underneath it.

The phonograph was between the Scar and Donahue who was sitting on the center loveseat with a woman. Both had their backs to the mystery man and both had drinks in their hands.

The Purple Scar checked his pistol, then pushed through the door.

The phonograph was in the middle of the room, playing Benny Goodman's new record, *Stompin' at the Savoy*, loudly. As he moved it, the Scar twisted the volume knob up to full.

The man turned. He was heavyset, with flabby jowls, the top of his head was bald, and his eyes were small and beady.

"Don't touch my record…"

He couldn't finish. The woman was on Donahue's left and he shoved her out of the way when he spotted the Purple Scar. The dame hit the floor, her robe billowing open. The Scar lunged over the couch, swung the top of his shoe into Donahue's jaw, and tackled him to the floor.

Donahue tried to smash his snifter of cognac over the Purple Scar's head, but the blow was deflected by his hat and the mask.

The Scar pinned Donahue, choked him down. Then he grabbed the woman, and dragged her around so she faced the full horror that was the mask of the Purple Scar.

"Go into the bedroom," he growled, "and lock the door!"

She tried to scream, but the Purple Scar slapped her throat. She gagged and dropped to the floor clutching her throat.

Donahue was struggling. He reached for the poker that hung next to the fireplace. The Scar swatted his hand away, grabbed the poker himself, and dropped the iron point of it into the flames.

"I've got a few simple questions to ask, Mr. Donahue," the Purple Scar growled angrily, "All I want is the truth. Give me that, and I'll leave."

Donahue kept struggling, petrified by the face of the corpse. Murdock had been meticulous when he'd rendered his brother's murdered and partially decomposed face.

The Purple Scar shifted, laid his knee on Donahue's throat. He began to apply pressure.

"Tap twice if you understand what I've told you."

Donahue kept struggling. He tried punching up at the Scar but it had been many, many years since Donahue had touched the hard labor that made his enterprise as strong as it was. He started in industry, working in an iron mine far outside the city limits. What used to be brute strength had gone away, and was now just useless flab.

The Purple Scar applied more pressure. A moment later, the mafia boss tapped his knee twice. He relented slightly.

"We're going to talk honest business. Yes?"

"Yes," Donahue croaked.

"Good. If you try and call for help, your life is forfeit. If you try and signal anyway while we're talking, you will die. Understood?"

"Yes."

The Purple Scar got up slowly. Donahue tried to do the same, but the avenger stopped him.

"No, you're going to stay there."

He slumped.

"O'Hara and Rebisi are about to go to war. Why would this benefit you?"

"My territory is caught in the middle of theirs. They'd fight on my turf. How does that help?"

"I've heard that you've been encroaching on O'Hara's territory."

"That's Rebisi's line. No one else says so."

"Lie," the Scar said, then grabbed the poker out of the fire, and dropped his knee across Donahue's throat again. The end of the poker glowed cherry red. The Scar held it above the mobster's eyes so he could see the glowing heat of it, then he shifted, lowered it slowly over the man's gut. Donahue couldn't see where the poker was now as crimefighter held it close to the his skin.

"Are you going to tell the truth?"

"Yes!" the mob boss croaked. The Scar lifted the poker, dropped the tip back in the fire.

"No, you're going to stay there."

THE PURPLE SCAR'S REVENGE

"Who stands to gain the most from a war?"

"I don't know. Whoever consolidated the most before this shooting began."

"If you were starting the war, how would you consolidate your business?"

"I'd get everything financial under my roof, start spreading money around to pay for weapons, munitions, medical supplies, and real-estate."

"So you'd organize the land-grab before you struck?"

"Yeah. Anyone who doesn't have a fixed target in mind when they go to war doesn't have a clear end-goal in mind. A war only works if it's fast, brutal, and ends before the cops can organize against you."

"If you'd made the preparations, how would you start the war?"

"I'd assassinate top-level bosses in the opposing family, then move on in the territory."

"Would you send your own guys?"

"Nah, that's too easily traced."

The Purple Scar considered this. O'Hara and Rebisi were both smart enough to play the preparation game like Donahue described. The question remained; would they be smart enough to contract out for the job of eliminating the enemy hierarchy before moving in?

"Who would you hire?"

"I wouldn't," Donahue said, "I've got a nice corner on Akelton. I wouldn't risk any of it."

"You're telling me that you're not involved in the war? That someone blew up the clinic in the slums for nothing?"

"As far as I heard, that was between Rebisi and O'Hara."

"As far as you know," the Purple Scar repeated then grabbed the poker, put pressure on Donahue's throat, and then held it over his exposed belly.

Gunshots rang out in the hallway. The Scar hesitated, the poker in hand, just over the mob boss's expanse of jiggly flesh. The double doors burst open, and a tall man in a black suit rushed through. The Purple Scar threw himself down behind the loveseat as a pistol roared. Donahue twitched as he was hit. Bullets tore into his face, chest, and torso killing him.

The Scar shoved upright, threw the poker like a long throwing knife at the attacker. He pulled his pistol as he did so. The man ducked from the poker, which hit the wall, and fired back.

The Purple Scar ducked, then leapt up again, and fired two shots at the assassin.

More gunfire tore into the loveseat. The Scar waited for his opportunity to strike back. He lowered himself to the floor, peered around the edge of the sofa. The man stopped firing for a moment. When the Scar twisted to take his shot, something landed on the body of Donahue. The Purple Scar hesitated, looking at the strange object.

It was a shrunken skull.

The attacking gunman rushed back through the double doors. The Scar snapped off several shots, but none hit the fleeing assassin.

The avenger stared down at the shrunken skull. It had dark skin, shriveled like wrinkled parchment, with white paint on the face, empty eye sockets, and short, braided hair.

He stooped, grabbed the skull by the small coil of string attached to it, and jogged towards the door.

The poker had landed amongst a pile of books and a fire started. It was spreading rapidly through the stacked volumes. He ran to the bedroom, kicked the door open. Inside was a woman; she screamed. He stuffed his pistol into his pocket, grabbed her by her robe, and dragged her towards the door.

The fire spread across the bookcases, was now tearing across the carpet. Benny Goodman's record had run out. The Purple Scar shoved the woman into the hall. The stair-well to the roof opened, and the guard that had gone up for his smoke returned, gun in hand.

The Scar pushed the woman aside, drew his revolver, and fired twice from the hip. The first shot went wide, the second winged the man in the upper arm. He fired again, and the man fell to his knees, then onto his back.

The woman ran for the stairs, burst through the door, started to descend. The Purple Scar ran after her; not to catch her, just to escape. She screamed as she went, "Fire! There's a fire!"

As he went through the door, he pulled his mask off, and hid it in the secret pocket of his coat. He slid the shrunken skull into his coat as well.

As he approached the bottom of the stairs, several other people moved behind him. Workers for Donahue, burning the midnight oil.

Out in the lobby, a police car was responding to the scene. It slid sideways in the street, and cops threw the doors open. They stood behind the doors for cover, their guns drawn.

Murdock came through the door behind an older businessman.

"It's a fire!" Murdock yelled, "Get the fire trucks!"

The cops' demeanor changed. The cop on the left reached into the car, grabbed the receiver, and called it in. The other cop ran towards the building to make sure everyone got out okay.

Murdock kept walking, his hands in his pockets. He crossed the street, went to the phone booth, and stepped inside. He called home.

Tommy Pedlar answered.

"Murdock residence."

"Hey, Tommy," Murdock said, "I need a favor."

"Name it."

"I need ya' to wake Professor Hamilton. Tell him I'll be there in a half hour with an urgent consultation request."

"I'll make the call as soon as we're done here." Pedlar said.

"Great. Then I need you to come pick me up."

"Where are you?"

"I'll be at the corner of 33rd and Stout. Got it?"

"Sure thing. I'll be ten minutes, probably less."

"Good." Murdock hung up, and set to walking.

Professor Leonard Hamilton lived in a broad estate on the outskirts of Akelton. It had tall stone walls for a perimeter, broad weeping willows on the east end of the grounds, and in the center, it looked like a mansion lifted out of the English countryside and deposited squarely in the middle of the United States.

Tommy Pedlar drove a Ford. The drive over had been a detailed recap of the evening's events, starting with the burning of the clinic, culminating with his face-to-face with Donahue before the latter was murdered.

"Did you really stick 'im with that fire poker?"

"No," Murdock said.

"You should have," Pedlar said. "The fat bastard's caused a lot of pain."

"And Rebisi and O'Hara are innocent, are they?"

"You know what I mean, Doc."

"No, Tommy, I don't think that I do. All three of them are vile and bitter men."

"So why not help O'Hara and Rebisi go the way of Donahue?"

"Because this sort of crime is like a weed," Murdock said. "You have to pull it out at the roots else it'll just keep cropping up, and multiplying as it does."

"So what do we do now?"

"Find out who started the war. They'll have hired the assassin, who's now escalating things. We kill the assassin, the boss who's running the killer no longer has leverage; he can be cornered and prosecuted. Then the war stops."

"It sounds so simple in theory," Tommy said. He angled the old Ford around the bend, up the gravel drive to the front of the house. He eased to a stop, the brakes squeaked softly as he did so.

Murdock climbed out, his whole body ached. He limped to the front door of the Professor's mansion, rang the bell. It swung open a moment later, and Professor Hamilton stood there in a plaid robe, unkempt hair, stubble on his chin, and a sour expression on his face.

"Five hundred and twenty minutes," Hamilton said angrily. "Do you know what that means?"

"You sleep for eight and two thirds hours," Murdock said.

"Yes. Do you know how I get when someone aborts my five hundred and twenty minutes of uninterrupted sleep?"

"Irritable," Murdock hauled the shrunken skull out of his pocket, "but this appears to be genuine, and I figured it'd be worth waking you up."

Instantly, the man thawed. His eyes went wide as he hobbled forward, and gingerly grasped the shrunken skull in his hands.

"How very interesting," the man said. "How interesting indeed."

"I need to know where it came from."

"Well, for now I can tell you that this was a skull shrunken very specifically with voodoo. I can already tell by the lesions here, along the back of the cranium."

He walked away, and Murdock followed. He closed the door behind them. The old Professor went straight up the library-office on the second floor. It was a vast room, filled floor to ceiling with old books. A giant oaken desk was against the wall, a window opposite it. A bronze globe with the continents etched into its soft metal surface was in the center of the room. A fireplace was against the farthest wall, but the fire that had been burning in the hearth was just embers now.

The Professor sat down at his desk, clicked on a lamp, grabbed an over-sized magnifying glass, and began to inspect the skull.

"How did you come across this," the Professor asked.

"The police asked me to consult on a peculiar case," Murdock lied.

"Why you?"

"You've seen my own study at home."

"Ah, yes, your fascination for the history of hunters and the way they went about stalking their prey."

"Precisely."

"Still, it was wise of you to come to me."

Hamilton had an English accent, adopted no doubt from his many years studying the world in the company of an English archeological team.

"This skull bears some very interesting markings," the Professor said.
"What kind?"

"It would seem that whoever made this skull did so with the intention of cursing someone. I deduce that by the pigment used to paint the face, the crude way the skin has been preserved, and the way the jaws were sewn together."

"Any idea where it originated?"

"I know of a particularly violent sect of voodoo native to the lower eastern quadrant of the United States. Louisiana, in point of fact. This sect doesn't have a large following, per se, but it is a pesky one. Louisianan authorities hunt any trace of this gang with great enthusiasm."

"Is that really the word you want to use?" Murdock asked.

"No, you're right. It's more like zeal. They've gone insane in a small way to find and punish this sect. Wherever these voodooists go, much violence and bloodshed is sure to follow. I believe the Louisianans have even gotten the Federal Bureau of Investigation involved in the hunt. That was what I'd last heard, at any rate."

"Can you help me narrow this down?"

"I can't give you dental records of the man who shrunk it, but this skull was made in a very particular fashion. I'd be highly surprised if this was the only one of its kind."

Murdock's had an idea what to do next.

"Thank you, Professor."

"Do you mind if I hang onto this for further study?"

"I think it'd be best if I returned it to the police. Do you mind if I use your telephone?"

"Please, help yourself."

Murdock left the library. There was a telephone on a table set against the wall nearby. He picked it up, dialed Akelton's central police headquarters.

"Akelton Police Department," the operator said.

"Patch me through to Captain Griffin of Homicide, please."

"One moment, sir."

A moment later, Griffin picked up.

"Homicide, Griffin."

"Dan, I've got something I need your help with."

"Donahue's dead," he interrupted. "Would you have anything to do with that?"

"I didn't kill him."

"I didn't say that you did. Only that someone has and now O'Hara and Rebisi are fighting to divide up Donahue's land."

A small idea suddenly flickered in the back of Murdock's mind. He went silent to contemplate it. A moment later, Griffin interrupted Murdock's thinking.

"You still there?"

"Yeah, yeah, listen, do you have any unsolved cases where someone was killed, and a shrunken skull was left on the body?"

"Yeah. I've got six of those in the past two months. Why? The FBI is officially in charge of those cases, you know that right? They want to stop the war, too."

"No kidding. Listen, I've got a lead. It's a damn good one too; one that I think will put a bull's eye on who's turning these wheels."

"Do you care to elaborate?"

"In person. Not over the phone."

"Alright. Come on down to the station. And bring the skull. I'll need it in evidence if we're going to make a righteous conviction out of any of this mess."

"See you in twenty," Murdock said, and hung up.

He went back into the library, collected the skull, bid the Professor a pleasant night.

+++

Captain Griffin had a small black board in his office. The six files were laid out on his desk. Murdock had drawn three columns on the board, with three rows. The columns were labeled 'Rebisi, Donahue, O'Hara' while the three rows were labeled 'importance; low, medium, high.'

"So this is your bright idea?"

"Damn right it is. And it's a good one, too."

Murdock looked at each file, then put a hash-mark on the board. It took him twenty minutes to sort through all the information that had been compiled, but when he was done, pieces of the puzzle began to click into place.

"What is this?"

Murdock gestured to the "high" row on the board.

"Tonight, high-level employees of Donahue were murdered in the clinic. That started tonight's festivities. But I don't think that was a hit, at least, not one that was contracted to our Shrunken Skull Killer. But last week, an important book-keeper for Rebisi was knocked off. Before that, a low-level enforcer for O'Hara. And the pattern continues, except with one inconsistency."

Murdock tapped the low-level enforcer that had been killed.

Captain Griffin's eyes started to widen as he began to connect the dots. Two dead for Donahue, three dead of Rebisi, and one man died for O'Hara.

"It'd be almost too obvious if only men from two of the three families were dropping dead. Everyone could put that together. But with employees from all three families falling, it kept the war at the brink because no one wants to start a pointless fight with the wrong man."

"Exactly. To divert suspicion with the simple fact of 'we're being attacked, too,' which kept the likes of Rebisi and Donahue from getting too trigger happy and smashing up one of the other families."

"So what? The low-level guy killed in O'Hara's gang were for what, exactly?"

"A down payment. Deniability in orchestrating a gang war the likes of which Akelton has never seen. The ground work has been laid, and it culminated with Donahue's murder tonight. The final body dropped, and now O'Hara can move in, seize control of the industrial assets of Donahue, and he's got control of the overwhelming percentage of Akelton."

"But what about Rebisi? The man's not an idiot, even if he is blood-thirsty."

"He's having to make his shopping list of property on the fly. And he's behind the curve. O'Hara would have been notified the minute that Donahue was dead, so he could move in."

"So what do we do?"

"We take a day, and tomorrow night see what O'Hara's put his name on, and what he's centralized his forces around."

"Great. So for twenty-four hours Akelton burns?"

"Not exactly. I'm still after the hit man. If I can corner him, put him down, then O'Hara's threat disappears. He's still dangerous, he's still got lots of goons on hand to throw lots of lead downrange, but he doesn't have the hidden spear that can reach out and kill whomever, whenever. It may still stop the war."

"Captain?" A young cop ran into Griffin's office. "We're getting reports about an extended gunfight out at Akelton Iron Works."

"You called it," Captain Griffin pointed at Murdock, "but they're twenty-four hours early."

"Yup. Now the question is; where are the Bosses?"

"Rebisi will be around to supervise his end of the fight."

"And that means that O'Hara will be there to make sure things go according to plan."

"Keep me posted," Griffin said to the younger cop, who then ran back to the dispatch stations on the other end of the floor. Griffin looked at Murdock. "Are you getting into the fray?"

"I am," Murdock said, "As the Scar."

"Do you have a plan?"

"I do indeed," he smiled at Griffin. "It'll work, Dan. And it'll be over before sun-up."

"That's three hours. You better be right."

Murdock shrugged.

"If nothing else, we just shoot all the bad-guys, and get mean with anyone who tries to start the mob up again."

Griffin nodded, walked from his office. Murdock followed downstairs. On the way, they passed through the armory where a dozen other cops were gathering shotguns.

Captain Griffin forsook his Ford at the curb of the police station for a police van full of cops being loaded in front of the Ford. Murdock hesitated next to the car. The city's lights cast a reflection back onto the low clouds. A moment later, the first few drops of rain began to fall. Murdock thought that was appropriate.

"Let's do this," Griffin said.

Griffin climbed into the back of one of the four police vans, and Murdock followed him. It set off a moment later, and sped out of the city, the siren wailing.

+++

It took almost an hour to get from the center of Akelton to the mine. As they approached, Captain Griffin hammered on the bulkhead between the driver's compartment and the back and yelled, "Siren off!" Silence fell through the valley, save for the sound of the rain on the metal walls and the sound of the engine.

Three minutes later, Murdock heard the echo of gunshots. He pulled his revolver, checked the load, and kept it handy. The cops around him primed their own weapons. Captain Griffin took a deep breath and said, "Here we go."

Murdock nodded slowly. The police van lurched off the paved road, and found dirt. The roar of gunfire was closer now, much more pronounced.

"We'll run in!" Griffin yelled. The van stopped, and the back doors opened.

Murdock rushed out with the policemen.

Two dozen cars had converged on Akelton Iron Plant. Men were hunkered down behind them, shooting at the other mafia men. Several bodies were on the ground. Tall light poles shone light on in the middle of the yard. Some of the lights had been shot out. The sun started to rise, but its illumination was muted by the clouds overhead.

The gunfire shifted from shooting at each other to shooting at the incoming cops. Bullets tore into the van, and off the tall fence that surrounded the property.

Captain Griffin ran towards the heavy metal gate which had been slid aside. He took cover behind it. Bullets pinged and whizzed off the hard metal, but none went through.

"How do we do this?" Murdock yelled.

"Don'tcha think we should've addressed that question before we got into the fight?"

"Probably."

The other police vans rolled up. They slowed, the cops piled out of the back, and Griffin waved the vans forward. The first one crept along towards the front gate slowly. The driver kept his head down as bullets tore into the glass. It shattered a moment later, but the van kept rolling. The cops began returning fire around the edges of the van. The van's headlights were shot out, one after the other.

In the sudden and complete darkness near the gate, Murdock got an idea. He turned, and sprinted off towards the left, inside the yard. He ran as hard as he could, dove behind a parked car with no one behind it, and took cover. Griffin followed a moment later.

"Time to make an appearance," Murdock said, then pulled out the mask of the Purple Scar. He dragged it onto his head, got it situated properly, then looked around again.

More police vans were moving in to start pushing the mobsters back. A half-dozen men near the building itself leapt up, and fired Thompsons at everything that moved. The Scar saw O'Hara run into the mining building. He snapped up, aimed his revolver, and ripped off a couple of shots. One body-guard fell as the others rushed into the building.

A moment later, some of Rebisi's men jumped up and escorted their boss along as well.

"You can handle these guys outside?" the Scar asked.

"Probably," Captain Griffin said. Murdock nodded, then rushed forward.

He sprinted to the next car. As he rounded the trunk and came along down the side, the mobster that had taken cover their lifted his pistol. The Purple Scar fired from the hip, jerked the trigger twice. The man fell limp.

Murdock rushed out with the policemen.

He ducked behind the car as slugs were tossed his way.

Bullets sent sparks up off the hood. The Scar flinched, looked up. Two men were shooting at him from behind a Buick with suicide doors.

The Scar fired again but his revolver clicked on an empty chamber. He dropped it, grabbed the dead man's pistol. It was a .45 automatic. The hand cannon roared, bullets tore into the body work and the goons flinched.

The Purple Scar looked around quickly. There was a light pole that still cast illumination between him and the next piece of cover, which was a stack of iron girders.

He shoved to his feet, sprinted across the open ground, and slid in behind the stack of metal. It rang loudly, hummed as bullets pelted it.

He crouched, slid to the corner, and looked around the edge. The two gunman he'd shot at earlier were now shooting at the cops. They had more lights on than could be shot out, and moved quickly into the yard.

He lifted the .45, squeezed the trigger. The gun roared, the first man jerked upright and tumbled back into his companion. He squeezed the trigger again; the man rolled off his buddy and hit the ground. A third trigger pull, and the second man fell over dead.

He rushed over, collected their pistols; one snub nosed .38, another .45 and rushed on towards the main building.

He slammed against the wall, peered around the corner. Dozens of bullets from a Tommy-gun tore into the metal of the wall, The Scar flinched, turned his head away. He took a deep breath, held it and waited for the man to reload. The gunman fell silent. The Scar twisted around the corner the .38 out in front of him. The crook was behind a Iron pillar, mostly covered. The crimebuster squeezed the trigger as he walked towards the man. Bullets pinged off the metal column, whizzed off into space.

When the sixth round went downrange, the man twisted, lifted his Thompson and the Purple Scar fired twice from the .45.

The pistol roared, the man staggered backwards, and went down. The Scar dropped the revolver, stuffed the .45 into his pocket, and picked up the man's freshly loaded drum-fed submachine gun. At the back of the downstairs lobby-office area with hardwood floors and metal walls, were two elevators. One was already out of sight. The Purple Scar ran into the other, dragged the gate down, and began his ascent.

The elevator jarred to a stop and the Scar found himself facing a wall.

"Get 'im!" a voice roared from behind him.

He twisted and saw that the elevator opened into a long metal tunnel. Huge boxes had been stacked against the sides for cover. The Purple Scar threw himself against the side of the elevator as bullets ripped into it.

He put the Thompson to his shoulder, then hooked his toe into the metal grate, and heaved it upright. He ducked under it, and crept forward slowly. A gunman leapt from behind the closest stack of boxes, sawn-off shotgun in his hands.

The Scar squeezed the trigger, sprayed the man in the chest with bullets. The gunman twisted as he went down, the spasm of death made him jerk the trigger. The gun roared and buckshot tore across masked man's arm as his foe went down.

The Purple Scar roared in agony and fell flat against the stack of boxes as more gunfire roared.

He looked at his arm. It was bleeding. He could feel several pieces of buckshot under his skin. But his hand still worked. He gritted his teeth, put the Thompson around the corner, then looked down the sights.

He saw one gunman with another Thompson firing down at him. He was crouched, the gun chattered spraying bullets into the stack of boxes behind him. The Purple Scar squeezed off a burst and the man was thrown backwards.

The gunfire lulled suddenly and the Scar heard Rebisi scream, "Stop that bastard!"

He saw the mafia boss run across the back of the tunnel into the corridors of the Iron mine itself.

"Crap," the Purple Scar growled.

Shielded lights hung from the metal-ribbed roof. The Scar lifted the sights of the Thompson, squeezed a round off into one near the next stack of boxes.

The men beneath them yelled as the sparks fell on them. The Purple Scar rushed forward, the Thompson clutched to his hip. He sprayed bullets to the right, took down one gunman, then bashed the butt of the gun against the face of the next man. The thug grunted and staggered against the wall. The Scar grabbed him, dragged him forward, and stepped in behind him. The man had a pistol in a shoulder holster, and a short-barreled pump action shotgun.

"Don't shoot!" the man screamed as the Purple Scar pushed him forward.

The other gunmen looked out, saw their comrade, and hesitated. The grim terror pushed the hood forward, the Thompson's barrel resting on the man's shoulder. The gunman aimed at the Purple Scar and kept careful track of him as the two men moved slowly through the darkness into the next pool of light.

The closest men reeled as the light hit the mask of the Purple Scar; they screamed and backed away as fast as they could. They stumbled over each other, blocked their comrades' lines of fire.

The frightening Scar squeezed the trigger of the Tommy-gun and men fell as they clogged the hallway. Near the back of the corridor, those least affected by the terrible image that was the face of a corpse returned fire, hitting more of their own men before getting anywhere close to the walking nightmare.

Bodies fell left and right. The Purple Scar kept pushing forward. The gunman he was using as a shield began to flail about as bullets struck him. The Scar continued to push him forward and he tumbled to the ground. Then the Scar ducked behind a stack of crates and fired down the corridor.

The Thompson clicked dry. The Purple Scar threw the weapon aside and pulled out the automatic.

"Rush him! Take him out!"

The Purple Scar heard the pumps of shotguns being primed. He braced himself, stood against the wall of the corridor, and leveled his sights around the corner.

The first goon appeared running forward with his shotgun. The Scar squeezed the trigger and the gun bucked in his hand as the gunman's head snapped back.

Murdock shoved off the wall and rushed forward. He dove at the dead body and his empty hand scooped up the shotgun as he slid against the wall.

He stuffed the pistol back into his coat, pumped the slide on the Winchester shotgun, and put it to his shoulder.

"Get after him!" the second-to-last gunman yelled.

"I'm not here to die for that bastard!"

The Purple Scar rushed forward as a gun further down the corridor went off. The Scar saw a body fall and the last gunman lift his revolver at him.

The Purple Scar fired first. The buckshot tore into the man's chest and threw him down. He hit the ground hard, and didn't move.

The Purple Scar stooped, picked up the man's pistol, and walked on down the hallway.

A few moments later, as he moved from the exterior tunnels to the first tunnel into the mine, the sounds of the external firefight faded. But he heard shooting coming from *inside* the mine. A string of lights was pinned to the wall. Since these were the only lights on in the entirety of the mine, he assumed this was the path that O'Hara, and subsequently Rebisi were taking.

The Purple Scar kept the shotgun handy, moved as fast as he could remain cautious. He felt exhausted, his body felt heavier than normal, and a terrible, aching pain began to seep into his bones. It started at the point in his arm where he'd been shot, and moved down towards his hands.

I've survived all night, and now I'll die of tetanus, he thought grimly.

He heard a man screaming in the tunnel just ahead.

"No, wait! I'm on your side!"

Then there was a sound of tearing fabric, and silence. The Purple Scar rounded the corner, looked down the tunnel. Nothing moved, but there was a body on the ground. The Scar listened, but could only hear the sound of running water. At some point, an underground spring had been tapped whilst mining.

He came to an open area where much excavation had been done. A body lay on the ground behind an ore cart. The tracks ran sporadically throughout the cavern, away from the walls, all merging on a central set of tracks that ran straight back towards the freight elevators.

Murdock took a slow breath through his nose as he approached the body. He caught a whiff of something terrible, something rotten and decomposing. Something like putrefaction.

The man on the ground belonged to O'Hara's gang. That was evident by the thick-cut suit and the fedora. Rebisi's men favored slimmer, Italian cut suits.

The man had been stabbed twice in the chest, in the heart. The incision began just below the sternum and was angled upward. There was very little blood on the chest but after the man had been stabbed there, the throat had been slit.

O'Hara's assassin was back and he'd just turned on his master. A small realization suddenly dawned on the Purple Scar. He found the man's pistol; an automatic .38. He rushed down the next lighted tunnel.

The Scar passed another body, one of O'Hara's men. As the lights turned downward he came upon a manually operated elevator that went into the lower reaches of the shaft. There was another body on the ground, this time one of Rebisi's men, stabbed twice and his throat slit.

"So that's the grand master plan," the Purple Scar whispered to himself.

The elevator was at the bottom of the shaft, probably one hundred feet down. The mechanical winch used to bring it up was broken off, which left it disabled.

He looked around and found a coil of rope left nearby anchored to a heavy pin mounted in the stone wall. The avenger kicked the coil over the side. It almost touched the bottom of the shaft. He slung himself over the side and very slowly slid to the bottom.

When he came to the bottom of the rope, the Scar was still ten feet above the elevator.

He heard voices beyond, but could not make out the words. He pushed away from the wall suddenly, let go of the rope, and dropped straight down.

The Scar landed lightly on his feet. He saw a goon standing just beyond the open-walled elevator. The man turned upon hearing the Scar approaching.

The Purple Scar lunged forward and bashed the man in the throat. Then he dragged him backwards, wrestled him to the ground, then twisted as hard as he could on the man's head. The neck snapped, and the man went limp. The goon had a short-barreled Thompson with a stick-clip. The Purple Scar picked it up, moved beyond the elevator.

Up ahead he could hear voices and moved in their direction. Suddenly there was some gunfire, which reverberated through the tunnels. Then just as suddenly it stopped.

"Do you really think this is going to work?" O'Hara's familiar voice roared with all his considerable lung-power.

"When I come back with your heads," a second unfamiliar voice responded, "then yes, I think it will work."

"You have to kill us first!" This came from Rebisi.

Around the next corner, the Purple Scar saw a wide cavern with a domed ceiling. The roof was only fifteen feet high but the room was easily one hundred feet across. Huge columns with Iron buttresses at the top were spread throughout, holding everything up.

The Scar crouched in the darkness and watched.

Gunfire roared again, flashes of light from Rebisi as he pulled the triggers on his dual pearl-gripped revolvers.

"You can't kill us both!" O'Hara yelled. "We've got too many allies on the outside!"

"But none of them are here now, and when death is the only power you have to wield, then I am your master."

There was a scream suddenly; a primal scream of pain and terror. It came from O'Hara. The mob boss twisted and fired his own customized Thompson for all he was worth but hit nothing of importance. In the dim light, The Purple Scar could see a knife sticking out of his O'Hara's back, off to the side. The wounded mobster reached around, tore the blade out and screamed in rage.

Rebisi reloaded quickly but did not shoot.

"I paid you a fortune!" O'Hara screamed.

"And you think this means I am beholden to you?" the third voice said. The Purple Scar assumed it belonged to the assassin; the one hired by O'Hara to start the gang-war of Akelton. The one who had attacked Doc Murdock's clinic.

"It means that you don't try and stab me in the back!" O'Hara roared, and opened fire again. He sprayed bullets around the cavern hoping luck would kill the assassin. The Scar couldn't see the paid killer, but it was obvious that he was skilled with anything that could be used to inflict pain and death.

A shadow darted off to the left. The Purple Scar saw the assassin slip around towards Rebisi. The Italian crook looked for the hired killer; looked for his opportunity to put the man down.

A gunshot rang out suddenly, and Rebisi slumped very slowly. The Scar saw a shadow rush forward and something gleam in the dim light.

Then Rebisi hit the ground and Murdock could see a crimson stain on his neck and shirt.

The assassin then raced towards O'Hara. The Purple Scar stood up, put the Thompson to his shoulder, and squeezed a burst. O'Hara screamed, but so did the assassin.

The Scar sprinted around to the right, trying to keep the assassin in view as he himself got to cover.

"Who's this then?" the man yelled. The Purple Scar looked down and saw O'Hara on the ground, unmoving.

"Most men call me the Purple Scar. I'm a bad man to piss off."

"Is that so?" the assassin laughed. "And what did I do that incurred your rancor?"

The Scar knew that as the cops took over the Iron mill they would soon be moving inside. He had no idea how far off they were and he didn't know who might hear his words.

"You attacked a friend of mine when you blew up his clinic."

"Oh yeah, huh," the assassin said absently. He sprinted to the left. The Purple Scar fired a burst, then ran to the right. The assassin returned fire, none of the bullets struck anywhere near the Scar. "That was actually a miscalculation. The clinic wasn't supposed to explode and I was told it would be empty."

"I thought you were more of a professional than that," the Scar countered, "than to take someone else's scouting notes at face value."

Gunfire rang out from the other side of the cavern. The Purple Scar kept to the right inching towards the assassin who had stopped moving.

With the Thompson to his shoulder, the Scar circled around the assassin. The man was reloading his gun but he was doing it slowly. The Scar guessed he must have hit the killer.

"It's a shame, really," the killer said. "I would've liked to have squared off with you properly. You've been dogging these bosses all night. I can only imagine how you'd focus on hunting a single man."

"You have no idea," the Scar offered. The assassin wheeled, surprised by the masked avenger's proximity. The Purple Scar pulled the trigger as the gunman also fired.

Something tugged at the Scar's coat as he stitched bullets into the killer's chest. The Purple Scar took a step and felt he strength desert him. He collapsed to his knees.

The assassin slid to the floor. His eyes were wide, and he stared at the Scar with surprise.

"How?" the man asked, then slumped over and died.

The Purple Scar took a slow breath. Terrible pain slashed across his torso. He'd been hit badly, he realized. With a painful effort, he dragged himself to his feet. He let the Thompson slide to the ground and hobbled along towards the tunnel mouth. He moved slowly towards the elevator.

He pulled his mask off as he came to the lift and stuffed it into his coat. He fell against the console with the lever. His legs felt weak, his lungs felt leaden. He couldn't take a deep breath. He realized he had a collapsed lung, maybe both were collapsed, and substantial internal bleeding.

In that moment, he regretted being a doctor, able to diagnose himself.

Miles Murdock threw the switch on the elevator and it began to rise slowly. He turned, tried to look up at the ceiling, but he couldn't. He slid down to his knees, then onto his back.

When the elevator came to a stop, he had no strength to pull himself out. He tried to move, managed to roll onto his stomach, when all strength abandoned him.

The darkness closed in around him. He tried to fight it, but couldn't. He let out a breath, and the darkness was all he knew.

Doctor Miles Murdock felt something. It was odd, really, considering that he didn't expect to feel pain in death. He felt a sharp sensation in his chest, working around near his heart, to the surface. He tried to move his hands to investigate, but other hands stilled him.

"He's awake," a female voice said and he recognized it immediately. Dale Jordan, his operating assistant. She was more to him than a mere assistant however; she knew the secret of the Scar and loved Murdock regardless his secret crusade.

"Well, Doc, that was close," Dan Griffin said.

So he wasn't dead.

"How--?"

"Captain Griffin found you," Dale explained. "He chased after Rebisi and O'Hara into the mines and found you in the elevator."

Murdock opened his eyes wide and looked around slowly. He realized that another doctor and a nurse were in the room as well, and so he couldn't talk about the mask inside his coat.

"You feel up to clarifying something for me?" Griffin asked.

"Do I have a choice?" Murdock croaked.

"No."

"Then go ahead."

"What the hell happened at the end there?"

"Ever read Mary Shelley's book?"

"No."

"Let me put it to you this way; O'Hara hired the assassin to help clear the playing field so he could make a power grab, and control the majority of Akelton, and eventually muscle Rebisi out of town. The assassin, however, got his own ideas, and went off on his own tangent. He figured that if he killed the three Bosses, the territory was prime for a new boss to control it all. That new boss would be him."

"Oh," Griffin grumbled. "That's not going to be easy to write up."

"None of it will be."

The doctor came over and checked Murdock's pulse and blood pressure, then said, "I must insist that my patient needs to rest."

"Then help yourself to the door," Murdock said.

The doctor rolled his eyes, but after a moment, did as instructed. Dale and Captain Griffin remained.

"The city is going to help you rebuild your clinic," Griffin said. "Since all the assets of the three families have been seized, they've all gone into the city's budget."

"That's great!" Murdock exclaimed, surprised at his good fortune. "It'll put the money to good use."

"Maybe," Dale said. She moved over and sat down on the edge of Murdock's bed.

"Thanks, Miles," Captain Griffin said. He pulled a cigar out of his pocket, lit it, and left the recovery room, puffing on it contentedly.

Murdock turned his eyes up to Dale. Her face was calm but her eyes were on fire.

"Let me explain..."

"No, let me explain," she interrupted him. "I took your jacket home. I burned it. Mask and all. The mob is dead and this city doesn't need the Purple Scar anymore."

"Just because the mobs have fallen doesn't mean that crime is gone. All those dirty cops? Who's going to deal with those? And what about the next guy who thinks he can come in and make the city into his own personal piggy bank?"

"If it comes to it, we'll talk about it then," she smiled fully aware she couldn't sway him for very long. "For now, I think that Miles Murdock, M.D. and Purple Scar both need a vacation."

He smiled up at her. He reached up and put a hand behind her head. He pulled her down so he could kiss her.

"I agree," he decided happily.

THE END

THIS ONE WAS TOUGH

In the many years I've been writing, few stories have been as difficult to pen as the Purple Scar piece you've just read. I wrote three drafts of the story, and struggled with it entirely. That being said, I'm glad to have written it.

The Purple Scar was an obscure character in the golden days of pulp and I feel truly sad about that; he's a fascinating character to write about. He's a walking contradiction; a doctor, all about doing for others and giving underprivileged people hope, and by contrast, this terrible figure that stands as a tool to purge corruption.

The Purple Scar is truly an interesting character. As for the story itself, well, that's a little different. I wrote a draft, a plan, that was a twisting, turning, knotted mess of a story that was utterly complicated and absolutely bewildering. I tried to untangle the mess to salvage something useful, and in the end, was given a very simple directive.

So I put that directive at the top of my computer, and wrote the story. When I finished the drafts, had them edited, I sent it to He Who Publishes, and promptly went to something that wasn't the Purple Scar. I realized something once the Scar story had gone fully from my mind and I was driving home from work one night. I figured out why the story was so difficult.

The Purple Scar, and Miles Murdock, had so much literary potential, and I had no idea how to wrangle that into a single story. That's what made the story so challenging; I was trying to ride a bucking, untamed Bronco cross-country. Not the best idea I've ever had, I'll be the first to admit it.

But that's it. The Purple Scar only got four stories back in the day, which is a crying shame. So much could have come from this character. I'm happy and grateful now that the Purple Scar has a chance to ride again through Airship 27.

Thanks for reading this. I'm always eager whenever I pick up a book and see an afterword by the author and he discusses the process that went into the writing of any given book/collection/anthology. Knowing how others ply their trade gives me inspiration to try and be a better writer myself.

But, as in a great many things, most of the time when someone writes, we're not dictating as much as we're just holding on for dear life and attempting to tell you what it's like to ride the bronco.

JONATHAN FISHER - is a young writer with big dreams who very recently stumbled into a bit of luck with his writing goals. This is his second story for Airship 27, and he is enormously grateful for the opportunity. His plans for the future include finishing the 19th draft of his novel, publishing a great many short stories, and buying an old Ford from a junk yard so he can go rallying.

LIQUID DEATH
BY GENE MOYERS

Dr. Miles Murdock was just shaking hands with a departing client when the square jawed figure of Captain Dan Griffin entered his waiting room. Square was a good word for Griffin who was not only square jawed but also square shouldered and fair and square in his dealings with everyone, all of which made him a fine homicide detective. With a last word for his client Murdock turned and shook hands with his policeman friend. While they shared similar black eyes, the husky officer was a bit shorter and huskier than Murdock's athletic six foot frame. His curly black hair and handsome good lucks gave him the appearance of a playboy but the clear look in the doctor's eyes and serious demeanor showed a man of strong character.

Smiling, Doc let go the hand and said, "Well, Dan it's good to see you, but what brings you out today. I'm not under arrest am I?"

Griffin laughed, "No, not today Miles. I was just passing by and thought I'd stop and say 'hello.' How's business?"

"Slow I'm glad to say. Business for me generally means traumatic injury for someone else." He eyed his stocky friend carefully, "But I'll bet you didn't stop by just to pass the time of day, did you?"

Dropping his voice Griffin motioned toward Murdock's inner office, "Actually if we could have a private word, I'd appreciate it."

Murdock nodded and led the way to his private office. Seating himself behind his desk Doc motioned toward the comfortable chair in front of it. When Griffin was seated Doc looked him squarely in the eyes, "So you're here on business. What can I do to help, Dan?"

"Well, it turns out there is a new source of drugs out there that may have connections to the medical field here in town."

Interested, Murdock leaned forward in his chair, "What kind of shady business could go on among doctors and hospitals?"

"I'm afraid every profession has an ugly side. It turns out that lately there has a considerable pilfering of drugs in several locations around the city."

"Narcotics?"

"Morphine certainly and other things as well, including a considerable amount of these new sulfa based drugs for infections. We are naturally worried about street traffic in any kind of narcotics but I suspect there may be more to it than that."

"Really, how so?"

"Well, the word has come down from Washington that the federal government is worried about smuggling of critical drugs overseas to Europe. And, with the shape things are in over there, what with the war in Spain and Hitler taking over Czechoslovakia they are definitely worried when drugs like these go missing."

Murdock nodded, "Everyone says that Poland is next. If a Europe wide war is about to break out every country is going to want to stockpile critical medicines like morphine and the new sulfa drugs, including ours."

Griffin agreed. He went on to tell Dr. Murdock that the police had been quietly investigating the theft of medicines from several clinics and hospitals for several weeks. They suspected that various staff members were pilfering the medicines and selling them on the black market. They had firm suspects and several arrests would be made very soon. He ended by asking Murdock to quietly do a comprehensive inventory of all his controlled drugs and take a good look at his personnel?

Murdock agreed even though he felt certain that everyone he employed was totally honest and his inventory was sure to be accurate. He also volunteered to check his incoming shipments to see that there had been no shortages. If he found anything, he agreed to notify Griffin immediately. The captain stood up, Murdock came around the desk to show him out. In the waiting room they again shook hands, "Thanks for you co-operation Miles, let me know how it goes."

Murdock stood thoughtfully for a moment and then turned and walked briskly down a short hallway. He looked into a small but tidy office but found it empty. He then moved further down the hall and pushed through double doors into his fully equipped operating theater. A tall, reddish-brown haired girl dressed in a nurse's uniform turned from an open cabinet. She had a towel in one hand and an odd shaped stainless steel object in the other, "Oh Miles, you startled me. I was just checking over the operating implements."

"Sorry Dale, I didn't mean to surprise you. I have something important that I'd like you to take care of right away."

Quickly businesslike she replied, "Of course doctor. What can I do?"

"I would like you to do a complete inventory on all our medicines, especially pain killers. I would like you to especially check our paperwork to be sure that we have received everything we ordered and that nothing was lost in shipment."

Dale frowned but nodded, "Of course doctor. Has there been anything reported missing?"

"No, and I'd like it to stay that way. Keep this just to yourself and report your findings to me only." He smiled disarmingly, "It's just a precaution, nothing to worry about."

He gave Dale an encouraging smile as he exited the operating room. Looking at his wrist watch Murdock noted that he had over a half hour until his next patient. Nodding, he made his way toward a stairwell and climbed quickly to his private quarters on the second floor. Once upstairs, he passed quickly through his comfortable living area, past his private study and entered his fully equipped gym. A familiar figure was tightening the mounts of a pommel horse with his back to Doc.

"Tommy? I have a job for you."

His aide and friend looked up and smiled, "Oh, hey Boss. What's up?"

"I want you to go out on the streets. I want you to hit up your contacts. Find out if there is any new source of painkillers out there, specifically morphine. Also ask around and see if there's any talk of black market drugs moving around. Got that?"

"Sure Boss, I'll get moving right away. Is this important?"

"Fairly important, get back to me as soon as you can."

"Right. It might take a while."

"I'll be here."

The rest of the afternoon passed quickly for Dr. Murdock. He was in his office after seeing his last patient when Dale knocked and entered. She passed him several sheets of paper, "Well, here is the inventory of every medicine and drug on the premises." Not looking at them he asked, "How did things look?"

"Everything matched. There is nothing unaccounted for. It balances down to the last gram and vial."

Murdock nodded, "Good, anything else?"

"Well, there was one shipment that we did not receive. We didn't pay for it though. Records show we reported the missing case and we weren't charged. The next statement shows the missing case was damaged in shipment and returned to the factory."

Interested Murdock inquired, "Where did that shipment originate?"

Dale consulted her notes, "Acme pharmaceuticals."

"Thank you Dale. What I need from you now is to go to the Down Street

Clinic tomorrow and do the same thing. Check everything very carefully."

"Fine doctor is there anything else?"

"No Dale, goodnight."

"Good night Miles," Dale gazed lovingly over her shoulder at Murdock as she closed the door gently behind her.

Up early the next morning, Murdock headed directly to the Down Street clinic. He spent a couple hours seeing patients and then made a point of helping Dale finish her inventory. They found nothing unusual. All drugs and medicines were accounted for.

Exchanging his white lab coat for his well-cut suit jacket he drove his roadster the few blocks to City Hospital. He first stopped to check on a patient that had been scarred in an auto accident. Dr. Murdock had operated on him and the patient was doing fine. Afterwards he stopped by the office of Dr. Johnson the administrator to see if he had any news about drug shortages. Sure enough, City Hospital had seen some shortages of critical, controlled medicines in the last few months. Lately they had been co-operating with the police and they had been notified that there would probably be arrests made very soon.

Thanking him, Doc left and was walking toward the main entrance when he noticed a tall, well-built man in a doctor's coat talking to an orderly just ahead in the hallway. There was something very familiar about the man even from the rear. As he passed the two he heard a familiar voice, "Miles? Miles Murdock, is that you?" Stopping he turned and looked into the handsome face of a young doctor not much older than himself. He knew him instantly: Graham Foster MD. He had met Foster in his first year at medical school. Despite being two years ahead of Murdock the two had become good friends. They had stayed in touch when Foster had graduated and gone on to specialize in infectious diseases and immunology. Murdock had lost touch with him in the last couple of years.

Murdock held out his hand, "Graham, it's good to see you. What brings you down to Akelton City?"

"I'm working here now at the hospital. Have been for a couple of months, I heard you were in town and I intended to get in touch but I've been frightfully busy." He turned back to the patiently waiting orderly and said, "You'll look into that matter and let me know what you find Mitchell?" The orderly nodded his agreement and left quickly.

Turning back to Murdock, Foster asked, "I've heard you have a successful clinic here in town and are doing some fine work."

Modestly Murdock nodded, "I have a free clinic on Down Street and I finance that with work out of my Swank Street office. I've managed to help a few people and am very happy here, but what about you? The last I heard you were up in Boston doing research."

Foster's handsome face darkened, "My research grant wasn't renewed. I tried for months to find other funding but finally gave up. Desperate to keep up my research I shopped around for jobs and finally wound up here in Akelton City. The hospital administration had heard of my research on anti-bacterials and offered me a staff position. I agreed as long as I had adequate time for research. But I'm afraid that even part time work on staff here will leave me little time for research."

"That's wonderful Graham. The hospital is lucky to have you. Does this research have something to do with Alexander Fleming's work? I know you studied under him for quite a while."

"Absolutely, I learned some wonderful things from Fleming. My research involves modifications to naturally grown anti-bacterials to make them more easily manufactured. If successful, it will revolutionize the treatment of infections."

Murdock nodded, "Important work. We should have lunch soon so I can hear more about it." Promising to make time for further discussion Foster excused himself to continue his patient rounds and Murdock left to drive home. On the short trip back to Down Street he mused about the coincidence of meeting his old friend so suddenly. Once back at his Down Street clinic he saw some patients then caught up with paperwork. Soon the phone rang; picking up the receiver he found it was Tommy. He had found out some information but wanted to speak in person.

Murdock passed the rest of the afternoon working at the Swank clinic. After closing he went upstairs to his living quarters and made himself a simple dinner. Soon enough the familiar figure of Tommy Pedlar, former "second story man" and confidential aide, entered the room. The two retreated to Murdock's study where he offered Tommy a drink and a seat. When settled he asked, "Well, what's the word?"

"You were right Boss. The word is there is a new source of morphine on the streets. No one knows where it comes from but the quality is said to be really good." Murdock nodded grimly. Yes, it didn't get much better than pharmaceutical grade, "Anything else?"

"Yep. There is talk on the street about smuggled drugs. The word is they're "hot" medicines coming from the hospitals in town."

"Any word on who's behind it?"

"I got a name, Max Snelling. He deals in stolen goods and people say he seems to know what's going on."

"Hmnn, does Snelling usually push drugs?"

"No. That's the thing. Snelling isn't known for that. He's a well-known fence but has never dealt in drugs before. I guess there's always first time though."

"How can I find him?"

"He moves around a lot. I don't know where he is now but I should by tomorrow. I'll let you know as soon as I find him."

After Tommy left Doc thought about the visit the Purple Scar would soon make to Max Snelling.

As Doc entered the Down Street clinic the next morning he found Dale Jordan and several of the staff gathered around the front desk reading the morning paper. "What's so interesting this morning?"

Giving him a questioning look, Dale handed him the front section. The lead story immediately drew his attention. It told of a series of arrests made by the police at various clinics and hospitals in the city. Apparently certain of the staff at these establishments had been quietly stealing drugs. A name immediately caught his eye. The article mentioned an arrest made of an orderly who worked at City hospital named Mitchell. Was this the same orderly he had seen talking to his friend Foster just yesterday?

Murdock spent the morning at Down Street and returned to Swank Street in the afternoon. He was in his office doing paperwork when Tommy called. He had located the fence Snelling and they made arrangements to meet that evening. Time passed quickly and by nine that evening he was in his private apartment making his preparations.

Going to his safe he quickly dialed the combination and opened it. He reached in and removed a limp rubber mask. Holding it up, he beheld its horrible appearance before slipping it into a concealed inner pocket of his long trench coat. He placed a set of master keys and a pencil flashlight in to the left hand pocket of the coat and after flipping open and checking the chambers, he slipped a short barreled .38 caliber revolver into the right hand pocket. Gloves and a hat pulled low completed his dress. Murdock then slipped out the back door of his apartment through the private alley entrance and made way to his parked roadster and drove carefully across town.

In a quiet neighborhood of tenements Doc coasted to a stop mid-way along a block to allow a lone figure waiting in the shadows to quickly enter the car. He then accelerated quietly away. Tommy then directed him toward a rather rundown part of old town. Parking the car near the corner of a block of mostly shuttered businesses the two exited the car and moved carefully down the darkened sidewalk. Doc could see that most of the small businesses on this block had gone out of business. Many storefronts were boarded up and few lights came from upstairs apartments. With half the street lights out, the street was cloaked in shadows. Grabbing Doc's arm Tommy whispered in the physician's ear, "There, just ahead in the old *Majestic* theatre building, our man has got a hideout in the backstage area. Snelling thinks no one knows about it. He only uses it when he's laying low."

"Is he alone?'

"Not sure. If he has anybody with him it will be only one bodyguard. Not many people know about this hideout. The word is, he's gonna blow town"

Doc thought a moment, "Entrance in the alley?"

"Yeah, the front is boarded over."

"Okay. I'm going down the alley. Give me a few minutes to get ready then make some noise at the front. Bang on the door. Make Snelling think that the cops are raiding the joint. When he rabbits out the back I'll get the drop on him. Then get out of there and meet me at the car."

Tommy nodded his assent and faded quietly down the street. Doc moved back to the corner and down the side street to the alley. Reaching into the hidden pocket of his trench coat he pulled out the flexible, form fitting mask modeled on his dead brother's terrible death face and pulled it over his head. Instantly he became the Purple Scar. Entering the alley he moved quietly along, the only noise his muffled footsteps. Reaching a point half way along the alley block he looked around. A narrow sliver of light showed under a door in row of buildings to his left. The Scar looked around but there was nothing big enough for concealment nearby. A brief flash from his pencil light revealed a nearby fire escape overhead. He started to jump up to grab the spring loaded ladder and pull it down when he thought about the horrible noise the rusty metal would surely make. Instead he moved down the alley to a discarded oil drum that smelled of its use as a garbage can. Lifting it, he carried the barrel back to the fire escape. Upending it, he climbed atop the barrel. Once there, stretching his arms upward and flexing his legs he jumped upwards and caught hold of a solid part of the metal framework. The Scar climbed up and settled himself on the lowest level of the fire escape, revolver and flashlight in his hands. The door he was watching was fifteen feet away.

He didn't have to long to wait. Soon there came to his ears distant shouts and loud banging. He was too far away to understand anything but it was apparent that Tommy was putting on a good show out in front of the theatre. Within seconds there came a sudden glare of light as the door he was watching burst open. The light streaming into the alley was dim but seemed bright after the blackness of the dark alley. Two men flashed into sight turning to run down the alley, both had guns in their hands. The Scar stepped over the low railing and dropped. It was twelve feet to the to the alley floor but the athletic Scar took it on flexed legs and came up with his pencil flash on and his revolver leveled. Caught in its glare were two men. One was a large hulking man in rough work clothing; the other was shorter and older wearing a cheap, wrinkled suit. Both held guns and tried to shield their eyes from the glare of the light with their free hands.

The Scar barked out, "Drop those guns! Hands Up!"

The larger man raised his gun and fired. The Scar dropped to one knee and returned fire. He felt the snap of his enemie's bullet going over his head as his revolver bucked twice in his hand. The big man grunted and staggered back as the Scar switched targets. His third shot crossed in midair with the bullet fired by the older man. The hoodlum's bullet whistled by harmlessly, not so the Scar's. It found its target and the gunman's gun clattered to the ground as he clutched his arm. He cursed and staggered to lean against the wall as his big companion collapsed to the filthy alley floor.

The Scar advanced cautiously, his flashlight pinning the helpless hoodlum, kicking the wounded man's gun down the alley as he passed. He stepped decisively up to the wounded gunman. His eyes were squinted nearly shut in the glare of the flash and he was sweating heavily; the sweat running down his unshaven cheeks and jowly neck. Blood oozed between his fingers as he clutched his wounded right arm. "What do you want?" his voiced quavered.

The Scar leaned his face down close to the sweating hood, close enough where his hideous visage was clearly visible in the back splash of the light and whispered in his hoarse voice, "I want the truth!"

Snelling's legs sagged as he whispered in terrified awe, "The Purple Scar!"

"That's right and if you don't want to get what your pal got, you'll tell me

The big man grunted and staggered back...

what I want to know," he briefly flashed the light onto the unmoving form of the second gunman and then back into Snelling's face.

"Wha. . . what do you want to know?"

"These new hospital drugs you're pushing, how many hospitals and pharmacies are involved? How is it organized?"

"No, you got it all wrong, mister. I'm not pushing drugs I'm just the middle man."

Scar shoved the still hot barrel of his revolver into the thug's neck and gritted through his scarred lips," Don't lie to me!"

"I'm not lying," gasped Snelling. "I'm telling the truth. I was just hired to receive the stuff and hold it until dealers picked it up."

Scar thought about this for a moment, "Who hired you?"

"I don't know. I only talked to him on the phone."

"You never saw him?"

"A couple times but only in dark places. He always wore a hat and stayed in the shadows"

"If that's all you can tell me, you're of no further use to me," the Scar clicked the hammer of his revolver back to full cock. Snelling's face went even paler, "No, don't! I can tell you more."

Scar hissed, "What?"

"Uh, he was tall and he talked like he was educated."

Interested now, Scar encouraged Snelling with another soft jab of his revolver barrel, "How do you know he was educated?"

"Well, he used fancy names for some of the drugs."

This *was* interesting. "What else do you know? Any of his contacts at the hospitals or pharmacies?"

"No. He never talked about them. He just had the stuff delivered to my warehouse. But I wasn't the only one he was dealing with."

"Who else?"

"I don't know but I know there was someone. Whenever a shipment came to me there was always more boxes of drugs on the truck that I never got. When I asked about it the goons would just tell me to mind my own business."

The Scar thought about this for a moment, "How were they delivered?"

The still sweating Snelling swallowed and replied, "In a big commercial truck. You know, a stake bed with canvas cover. And there was always a couple tough guys doing the deliveries."

Scar prodded him once more with his gun, "And how did you distribute the drugs?"

"I didn't. Dealers just showed up and took what they wanted."

"What did you do with the money?"

"I didn't take any money. The dealers sent it somewhere. I was just paid by this shadowy guy to house the stuff. Please mister, I'm bleeding to death here. I need a doctor."

The Scar played his light over the wounded arm and looked at it with a critical surgeon's eye, "You'll live." He stood up to go. "You need a doctor alright but not in this town. Get out and don't look back."

Snelling struggled to get to his feet complaining, "But I need a doctor now, I'll bleed to death."

Scar took three long strides back and again rammed the gun against the wounded gunman's nose, "I'm giving you a chance that you don't rate. Go now, and if I see you around Akelton again it will be the last time."

Snelling wordlessly nodded. The Scar turned and walked briskly to the alley's mouth. Tommy was waiting for him with gun drawn, "Everything okay boss?"

"It's good. Let's go."

The two quickly slipped into the roadster. Tommy drove while the Scar removed and stowed away his mask. "Find out anything useful Boss?"

"Yes I did." Doc was very thoughtful as the powerful roadster sped through the night.

Busy with patients at the Down Street clinic it was nearly noon before Doc found time to call police headquarters. He was told that Captain Griffin was out at a robbery call at Zenith pharmacy. Grabbing his hat, Doc ran for his parked roadster and made the trip downtown at a record pace. He pulled up near the shop. There was a squad car parked out front and Capt. Griffin was just coming out of the pharmacy. Doc and he greeted each other and Griffin briefed him on what had happened. Two hours before two armed men had entered the business and ordered the pharmacist to close the place. Once closed, the gunmen forced the owner to help fill a laundry list of drugs which they carried away in two large sacks. They left the pharmacist tied up but unharmed. He had taken nearly an hour to get loose and notify police. "Most troubling," Griffin confided to Doc. "I'm afraid since we have penetrated the network of onsite thefts these drug pushers have turned to more violent means to fulfill their needs. Now we have to be on the alert for armed robberies and perhaps burglaries as well. I'm ordering increased patrols around pharmacies and hospitals day and night."

Doc decided to take the Captain into his confidence, at least part way, "There may be more to this than just drugs for the street. I think there is an organized group other than just drug pushers behind this. We have to find out where these drugs are being taken to when they are stolen. Have you found out anything from the arrests you made?"

The burly captain shook his head, "No. None of the employees we arrested knew who they were working for. All got their orders by telephone and dropped their stolen goods in out of the way places. Money was received in the mail."

As Doc was about to ask another question, a young patrolman hopped out of his squad car and ran toward them. "Sir, just it just came over the radio. There's been a robbery at City Hospital. They're asking for you."

Griffin cursed under his breath and looked around. Spotting a police call box on a nearby telephone pole he strode briskly toward it. Opening it with a key on his key chain he spoke briefly, then hung up and turned to Doc, "A truck unloading a shipment of drugs at the hospital was hijacked by three armed men a few minutes ago. I'm on my way. Want to come along?" Murdock nodded his assent and within a minute they were in the Captain's car speeding toward the hospital.

Upon reaching the hospital they drove around to the loading dock. There a platoon of hospital officials, security guards and police had gathered. Wading into the crowd Griffin quickly brought order to the group. Snapping out questions and orders like machine gun bullets he soon had things in hand. He then briefed Doc, "Looks like a delivery truck pulled up and three armed men who had concealed themselves in the alley sprang out, knocked the driver unconscious and drove away before anyone could notify security or even think about calling us. Whole thing took less than a minute, a well-planned job."

As Doc was about to reply a patrolman ran up to Griffin to whisper in his ear. Doc took this opportunity to single out one of the hospital officials on the dock. Stepping up to him he questioned, "Can you tell me what company's truck was hijacked here?"

The man consulted his clip board and said, "Look like it was a shipment from Acme Pharmaceutical."

Doc raised an eyebrow at this, "Special shipment?"

"No, the standard weekly shipment."

Before he could ask further questions he saw Griffin motioning him over.

"We found the truck. Empty. No sign of the thieves," he grimaced.

"Where was it?"

"Warehouse district down by the port."

"Has anyone notified Acme Pharmaceutical yet?"

"No. I was going to make the call as soon as I got back to Headquarters but I think we should go take a look at this truck first."

Dr. Murdock smiled, "I have a better idea. I think we should go and talk to Acme personally."

Surprised, Griffin hesitated, "Acme is up in Chesterfield, that's quite a trip."

"True, but I think it'll be worth it, after all, all of these stolen pharmaceuticals come from some place. I think it might be best for us to start at the beginning."

Griffin thought about for a second and nodded assent.

✝✝✝

Chesterfield was a busy but smaller city upriver from Akelton City. They followed the highway along the river to Chesterfield. Once there it did not take long to find the pharmaceutical factory. It was a modern set of buildings on the east side of town. Security at first glance seemed good. The complex was completely surrounded by a chain link fence. They were stopped at the main gate and Griffin was forced to show his police ID to gain admittance from the armed uniformed guard. They drove to the headquarters building and parked in the visitor's parking lot. Once inside, a few more flashes of the badge gained them access to the office of John Kline the plant manager.

Kline greeted them cordially. As he shook hands Doc took stock of him. The plant manager was tall and well-built with a shock of blonde hair slicked back. He would have been somewhat handsome if he smiled but at the moment he looked out of his blue eyes from under a furrowed brow. Once seated in his comfortable office he spoke, "I'm sure you gentlemen are here about the incident this morning in Akelton City. Can you tell me anything about the condition of our driver?"

Surprised Griffin asked, "I believe he is fine Mr. Kline, just a good bump on the head. How did you learn of the hijacking, so quickly?"

"A hospital official called a little while ago. Do you have any further news?"

Griffin spoke carefully, "We have located the truck; unfortunately the contents had been removed. We are still investigating and hope for positive news soon. Do you have a list of the contents?"

Kline rummaged among the papers on his desk and handed a paper clipped group across the desk, "I have copies of all the invoices for today's deliveries." Doc reached across for them and flipped through while Griffin continued questioning the manager. There was to have been nearly a dozen deliveries that day. Amongst them were considerable amounts of crucial drugs including hundreds of vials of liquid morphine. Totaled, the shipments were quite valuable. Doc turned his attention back to the conversation.

"Yes, we have had to increase production to keep up with increased demand from Akleton City," Kline was answering a question from Griffin. "I've read of the recent arrests you've made captain. It explains why many of our customers have increased their orders recently."

Before Griffin could ask another question Doc cut in, "What about your security here? Have you increased it since these thefts have come to light?"

Somewhat surprised to hear him speak up Kline turned a keen gaze on Doc; "Our security is first rate here. It hasn't needed to be increased. And our inventory control is the best. I go over every bit of paperwork myself. No drugs are being stolen from this facility. From the sound of everything I've heard, it is this crime wave in Akelton City that is to blame."

Griffin bristled at this implied criticism, "The Akelton police is doing everything possible to control these drug thefts, sir. Why we…"

Doc cut in smoothly, "Captain Griffin and his men are the best in the business Mr. Kline. I'm sure they're doing everything they can to catch these thieves. I wonder if you might show us your shipping and security procedures, it might be very helpful."

This seemed to forestall any further arguments between Griffin and Kline who quickly agreed to Doc's request. He spent the next hour showing them the company's shipping and delivery arrangements. It was all very formal with lots of paperwork showing where every vial and bottle went. They even got a quick look at some of the modern lab equipment producing many new and traditional medicines. When questioned, Kline stated that the pharmaceutical lab was less than two years old. It was Acme's newest plant and the crown jewel in their chemical empire. Kline had been appointed plant manager while it was still being built and obviously took great pride in it. Finally he showed off their security arrangements and concluded with the loading of a truck that was leaving immediately.

Pointing to a uniformed guard supervising the loading of pallets on the truck Kline stated, "After this morning I'm assigning armed guards to each truck. It's regrettable but I think necessary."

Doc mildly inquired, "Is one enough?"

"This truck is going north. The next shipment into Akelton will have two armed guards."

If Griffin took this implied criticism wrong he did not show it. Instead he thanked Kline and led Doc back to his car. On the drive home he asked, "Well did you learn anything?"

Doc thought a moment, "It seems like a well-run business and Kline seems very efficient and serious."

Griffin nodded, "Efficient but arrogant." The rest of the drive passed quickly and they reached Akelton late in the afternoon. Griffin dropped Doc where he'd left his roadster. Ten minutes later he was back at his Swank Street clinic and apartment. Once inside he picked up the phone and dialed City hospital. A quick inquiry and a short wait brought his party to the phone. "Hello, Graham. Miles Murdock here. I'm just fine, thanks. Sorry to disturb you at work but I don't have your home number. Anyway I called to see if you could have dinner with me tonight. I'm so happy that you're in town now and I would like to hear more about what you've been up to lately. Good. I'll pick you up at the hospital at seven. Yes, see you then." He was just hanging up the receiver when Dale entered his study.

"Very bold. Making dates with pretty girls' right in front of me. Does this mean so little?" She smiled disarmingly as she coyly held up her left hand and wiggled her fingers making the light reflect off the diamond on her finger.

Doc smiled, "Darling, you know there's no other woman for me. That was an old friend from medical school that I'm going to dinner with, and actually I'd much rather it were you in this instance." He looked slightly sad.

"Why is that dearest?"

"I'm afraid he might have something to do with all these stolen drugs. I'm going to attempt to get at the truth without letting him suspect that I'm worried about him."

"Who is this old friend and why do you suspect him?"

"His name is Graham Foster. He's a brilliant researcher in new drugs to fight infections. He has recently moved here, just as these thefts were starting. And, he is in need of money to carry on his research. In fact I'm afraid he is a little bitter toward the medical field just now. So I need to find a way to rule him out as a suspect."

Dale took his hand and squeezed it while she gazed fondly into his eyes, "I'm sure you'll find he's innocent. He sounds like a good man."

Doc nodded, "He was. I just hope he still is."

+++

Dr. Graham was waiting outside the hospital as Doc Murdock pulled up in his car. Graham stepped in and they were off. Doc drove to a night club called the Play House. A busy place, Doc had spent some time here months before while solving a nasty murder. The staff remembered him and quickly found a table for the two physicians. The two old friends fell naturally into conversation. They began by reminiscing and gossiping about friends in the medical profession. When Doc turned the conversation to Graham's move to Akelton, the tall physician was profuse for his praise of the city and its environs. He wanted to know all about what Murdock had been up to and Doc had to be careful to confine talk to his medical work and not seem to know too much about crime in the city.

Finally Doc asked, "Tell me more about your research work?"

Graham's face lit up, "I tell you Miles, the work on anti-bacterials is on the verge of some major breakthroughs. I was doing some wonderful work on synthesizing some of the ones found in nature. If we can do that, cost will come down and availability will skyrocket."

"Sounds like important work."

The smile on Graham's face faded and his countenance darkened, "Terribly important. That's why it was so disheartening to lose my research funding. Those short sighted Washington bureaucrats don't understand. They say we're still in a depression and tax money is tight."

Doc nodded agreeably, "That must be terribly frustrating."

"You don't know the half of it. I believe war is coming and if I'm right, production of these new anti-bacterial drugs will be crucial. I just can't make anyone understand how important my research is." A hesitation, "I'm sorry Miles. I don't want to sound bitter. After all, I'm sure you're the one man who understands just how important my work is."

"I do Graham. In the work I do with burn victims infection is a huge problem. These new drugs would be of immense help. Perhaps I can write some colleagues. If I can get a few people looking perhaps we can locate some new funding."

"That would be a big help Miles. I'm at my wits end. I'm desperate to get back to work on my research. The hospital has been good about letting me do some research on the side but I have responsibilities to my patients and there are only so many hours in a day. If only I could afford my own lab and assistants"

The rest of their conversation was overshadowed by an air of gloom from Dr. Foster. After dropping Foster at his apartment building Doc drove straight home. Once there he thought things over. His discussion with Foster had not gone well. He was angry and depressed but was it enough to drive him to illegal methods of funding? Possible. He was disturbed by a door slamming. Soon into his study strolled the familiar form of Tommy Pedlar. "Hey Boss, what's up? Anything new?"

"Hello Tommy, I'm just trying to sort out these new tactics the drug ring is using."

Tommy nodded, "You mean the hijacking. Heard about that."

"And the robbery at Zenith pharmacy."

Tommy seemed surprised, "Didn't hear about that. Say, isn't that place owned by a guy named Russelli?"

Doc shrugged, "I'm not sure. Why, is it important?"

"Well, when I was asking around about hot drugs on the street the Zenith pharmacy's name came up. Word was, if you needed something really bad you went to the Zenith. Supposedly this guy Russelli was very accomodating."

"Really. Why would a legitimate pharmacist be doing that."

"I asked the same thing and the word is that this Russelli likes the ponies. He's got IOUs all over town and is hurting for money."

Doc thought for a moment and then stood up. Going to his hidden wall safe he spun the dial to quickly open it.

Tommy watched with interest, "Is this Russelli guy going to get a visit from the Purple Scar?"

Doc quickly stashed his flexible mask away in its secret coat pocket and secreted several useful objects about his person. "He's on the list, but first we're going to make another call. Get the car." Tommy smiled and trotted happily away.

Traffic was light on the dark road to Chesterfield and Doc's powerful roadster made good time with Tommy behind the wheel. By the time they reached the Acme plant it was just after midnight. There seemed to be quite a lot of activity around the plant and parking lot for so late an hour. Doc had Tommy drive past the main gate and further along to place where they could park the car near the fence and observe. It came to Doc that it

"Isn't that place owned by a guy named Russelli?"

must be the closing time for the evening shift. It was unusual that a factory would have enough business to justify a second production shift in these tough economic times.

Realizing that this was the perfect time to make an entry Doc quickly drew out his flexible mask and slipped it over his head. Miles Murdock disappeared and was replaced by the Purple Scar. He next drew another mask from his pocket and slipped it over the first mask. This mask had the common place features of a very forgettable face. A hat on his head pulled low completed his disguise. He left Tommy orders to wait for him then turned and quickly scaled the fence. Once on the other side he moved across the open area into the parking lot. Tired workers leaving the plant and starting their cars or walking toward the main gate to catch buses paid him little attention. Once out of the open he made his way between buildings to the administration building he had entered earlier with Dan Griffin. Ignoring the main doors he quickly located a side door. It was locked but his set of master keys made quick work of it.

Once inside he oriented himself quickly. He wanted the second floor office of Kline the plant manager. Though the lights were turned down low there was still plenty of light to find a stairwell. Making his way to the second floor he quickly found Kline's office. He was trying the third of his keys in the lock when he heard slow footsteps coming from around a corner of the corridor. He tried a fourth key. No good. The footsteps came closer. He was beginning to sweat as he tried the fifth key. Finally the lock yielded. He opened the door and slipped inside just as a uniformed night watchman came around the corner. The Scar leaned against the door until the guard's footsteps faded down the hallway. Pulling his pencil flash he crossed to the inner door. It too was locked and it took four keys to find one that worked.

Safely inside Kline's private office the Scar set to work. He opened Kline's file cabinets and began sorting through paperwork. It was slow work and time passed. There were plenty of records almost all routine. Nearly an hours' worth of searching and all he could really conclude was the plant had started producing an unusual amount of certain key drugs a few months ago. More interesting was a file of personal correspondence between Kline and the home office of Acme Pharmaceutical. In response to inquiries Kline stated that his increased purchase of raw materials and production of key drugs was due to increases in orders from various Akelton City customers. He cited conversations with customers regarding shortages in their inventories.

Scar then moved to Kline's large desk. It was locked but yielded quickly to his master keys. A quick search revealed nothing out of the ordinary. Then he noticed the daily desk calendar. Nothing was listed for today but when he flipped to tomorrow's date he saw a neat notation:

Andrea Toroni 6:30

Flipping back through the calendar he found only routine notations until he came to a date almost a month before:

Hilda Neumark 9:30

The Scar frowned under his mask. Was Kline a ladies man? He certainly hadn't given the impression of being anything but a very serious, almost driven man. Perhaps he wasn't paying as close attention to his business as he had seemed. No telling what was going on under his nose.

Scar froze as he glimpsed a light under the door connecting with the outer office. He immediately killed his light. Tearing off his outer mask he stuffed it into his hat sitting on the desk. Picking up the pen light he glided silently around the desk. He was two strides away from the door when it swung open. A security guard stood in the entrance, one hand on his holstered gun. The startled guard's flashlight caught the Purple Scar's hideous features squarely in its beam. He opened his mouth and while he didn't quite scream like a little girl he certainly let out a startled sound that came out half gasp, half squeak. He didn't have the chance to make any other sounds as The Scar stepped strongly forward putting all his weight behind the straight right fist that caught the guard squarely on the jaw. His flashlight, flung from a numb hand, went out as its bulb shattered so Scar heard but did not see the guard's unconscious form hit the floor.

Quickly closing the hallway door he grabbed the guard's legs and dragged him into the inner office. Grabbing his hat and outer mask he quickly left the office. He saw no other guards as he made his way out of the building. Moving briskly among the buildings and across the parking lot he made his way toward the far fence where Tommy was waiting. He knew that the guard would regain consciousness soon and he wanted to be far away before an alarm was raised. He heard alarm bells begin to ring as he was climbing the perimeter fence. He threw himself into the idling roadster and nodded to Tommy who threw the car into gear and sped away.

Removing and stowing away his mask Doc filled in Tommy on the events at the plant. When finished he asked Tommy, "Have you ever heard of two women named Andrea Toroni or Hilda Neumark?"

Tommy thought briefly and shook his head, "Doesn't ring any bells." Doc was silent with his thoughts for a time. There was no evidence that Kline was behind these drug thefts but his plant or at least its products seemed to be at the heart of whatever was going on. Was it possible that Graham Foster was involved? Doc didn't like to think so, but it was quite a coincidence that these drug involved shenanigans had begun about the same time that Foster had moved to Akelton City, plus he did have an urgent need for money and he harbored some bitterness toward the medical establishment. Doc shook his head. It was sad that he was forced to suspect an old friend. And, what about this shady pharmacist Russelli? He would bear a closer look.

Doc's musings continued until they reached the outskirts of Akelton. It was late and as they motored quietly through downtown the streets were almost empty of traffic. Regardless, Tommy drifted to a stop at a red light. As they waited at the empty intersection they gradually became aware of a distant siren growing louder by the second. Glancing into the mirror Tommy proclaimed, "Not behind us."

Doc raised his voice over the growing howl of the siren, "From the left." As he said this a vehicle roared into sight traveling at high speed down the deserted street. It was closely pursued by a prowl car siren howling, its spotlight trained ahead on the vehicle it was pursuing. The first vehicle was a large, dark panel truck traveling without lights. One of the rear doors had not been properly closed and swung back and forth in time with the swaying of the truck as it raced down the street. Tommy looked expectantly at Doc. He nodded, "Go!" Tommy cranked the steering wheel, stomped on the accelerator and the powerful car fishtailed into the intersection.

The patrol car and panel truck were a block ahead but the powerful roadster rapidly closed the gap. As they drew up just forty feet behind the pursuing police vehicle flashes of light came from the darkened interior of the panel truck. Someone was shooting through the open rear door. The squad car began swerving to and fro to spoil the aim of the unseen gunman while one of the officers attempted to lean out the passenger side window to get off a shot in reply. Before the officer could take aim several shots seemed to strike the prowl car. Its spotlight shattered and went dark and immediately it swerved, jumped the curb and struck a mailbox. As Doc and Tommy rocketed past they saw the blue and red box arc through the air and go right through the plate glass window of a furniture store. The police car then struck a parking meter and came to rest against the side of a building. As Doc twisted to look at the police car he could see it was not badly damaged but he could not see if the policemen were alright.

Tommy swerved around the vehicle and closed the gap with the fleeing truck. Doc bent low and tugged on the mask with his dead brother's face and pulled his revolver from its holster. As they came up behind the truck he yelled loud enough to be heard over the roar of the powerful engine, "Get alongside so I can get a shot at a tire." Tommy nodded and swerved out across the center line. The Scar leaned out his side and drew a bead on the left rear tire of the speeding truck. As he fired three well aimed shots, sudden flashes and a rapid series of bangs came from the rear door of the panel truck. With a start, Scar recognized that whoever was inside was using some kind of automatic weapon. Three things happened simultaneously at this point; the truck's rear tire blew out and shredded throwing it into a slide, a burst of gunfire struck the hood and windscreen of the roadster and Tommy cursed as the roadster swerved toward the left side of the street. The Scar dropped his revolver and grabbed for the wheel. Tommy, clutching his left shoulder was falling toward the door. Reaching his foot across the car Scar stabbed at the brake while attempting to steer the out of control vehicle. Brakes and tires screaming the roadster jumped the curb, just missed a telephone pole, struck another of the ever present parking meters and came to rest against the wall of a magazine stand crunching in one wooden wall.

Pennies and nickels showered around the damaged car as Scar jumped to Tommy's aid. Pulling a handkerchief out of his pocket he tore open Tommy's shirt and pressed it to the wound in his shoulder. "Press this hard," he said placing Tommy's hand over the handkerchief. He grabbed his wrist and quickly took his pulse. While he did this he looked around. The panel truck was on its side fifty yards down the street. One rear door lay on the ground, the two now upper wheels slowly turned. Tommy's pulse was strong and his eyes looked clear. Grabbing his revolver from the floorboards where it had been thrown he whispered, "Stay here," and jumped from the car.

Holding his gun in front of him the Scar moved briskly toward the truck. When he was within ten yards of it a head appeared through the driver's side window and a man boosted himself out of the now overturned cab. "Don't move," barked the Scar. Half out of the door window, the man threw up his arms. He was dressed in workman's clothes and was bleeding from a cut above his eye. While covering the driver another gunman took this opportunity to roll out of the back of the open truck. He rolled along the ground and came up firing a wooden stocked submachine gun.The Scar dodged to one side firing as he moved. The automatic fire stopped suddenly and the shooter rolled onto his back his weapon clattering to the street. The Scar spun around but the driver had dropped over the front of the truck and was gone. Shaking his head Scar moved cautiously toward the shooter on the ground. Kneeling next to him he could see the man breathing but knew from his training that the man's wounds were fatal. He had only minutes to live. The Scar leaned down and in his hoarse whisper asked, "Who hired you? Who's behind this?"

The gunman couldn't go any paler but his eyes widened in fear, "The Purple Scar!" he managed to gasp out. The Scar grabbed his shoulder and was about to ask the question again when the gunman shuddered, rolled up his eyes and died. The Scar stood up. As he started toward the truck he glanced down at the gunman's weapon. Stooping, he took a good look at it. Although wooden stocked he did not see the expected large drum magazine of a Tommy-gun under the receiver, instead the weapon had a long magazine sticking straight out to the left of the gun. He looked up quickly as the sound of sirens came to him. Shaking his head he trotted toward his roadster. Tommy was conscious but looked pale. Pulling him gently from behind the wheel The Scar reassured him, "I'll get you out of here Tommy. You'll be alright." Slipping behind the wheel he started the engine, backed out, stomped the accelerator to the floor and disappeared down the street just as the first squad car turned the corner on the battle scene.

Driving without lights and dodging down alleys The Scar made a quick trip to Swank Street. By the time he parked in the alley behind his home, steam was coming from every crack and seam in the front of the roadster. Undoubtedly the radiator had caught one of the slugs flying at the car. He pulled off his mask and jammed it in his pocket. Gently lifting his wounded aide he carefully carried him into the clinic and directly to his fully equipped surgery. Placing Tommy gently on the operating table he began cutting away his shirt, "How you doing Tommy, any pain?"

"Not much Boss, it feels kind of numb."

Doc knew that Tommy was going into shock, the pain would come later. With the wound exposed he examined the shoulder carefully. Finally he told Tommy in a quiet voice, "The bullet's still in there. I'm afraid it's got to come out so I can close the wound and stop the bleeding." Tommy's face was pale as he nodded. Doc washed his hands and left the room to find a phone. Dialing Dale's number he quickly woke her. Giving rapid instructions he hung up and returned to his patient to prepare him for surgery.

Ten minutes later Dale came rushing into the surgery. She had dressed hurriedly and her hair was disarrayed but she still managed to look both competent and beautiful. Not for the first time Doc marveled at his luck. While Dale scrubbed her hands and pulled on sterilized rubber gloves Doc filled her in on the evening's activities. She made no comment but he could see the worry in her eyes. Not just worry for Tommy, Doc knew that she was imagining him there on the table waiting for a bullet to be removed. When she was ready, Doc signaled for ether to be administered and he began the operation.

Although specializing in plastic surgery Doc had seen his share of bullet wounds. His skilled hands went quickly to work and within minutes he had located the bullet and pulled it out. Dropping it into a stainless steel pan he quickly cauterized and closed the wound. After the operation, Dale helped him get Tommy into bed where he seemed to be resting solidly. Closing the door quietly they stepped into Doc's office and took seats.

It had been a busy night and Doc felt tired. It must have shown because Dale looked concerned as she asked, "What are you going to do now, Miles?"

He smiled back and said, "I'm going to watch over Tommy tonight and then tomorrow I'm going to follow up on some clues. This is getting out of hand and I've got to put a stop to it. But I'm going to need a little help from you, much as I hate to ask it."

"Ask anything you want, dearest."

"First, I'm going to need to borrow your car. I'm afraid mine has a lot of bullet holes in it and the trouble with bullet holes is that they look like just what they are. Then I need you to find out anything you can about these two women." He scribbled the names he had found in Kline's calendar down and handed the note to Dale. Glancing at the names she said, "Of course. One change though, I'll sit up with Tommy. You need your sleep, especially if you're going to have many more nights like tonight."

Doc quickly acceded to her wishes. When he mounted the stairs to his private apartment she was checking Tommy's pulse, the total nurse professional. Doc was asleep as soon as his head hit his pillow.

When he awoke refreshed late the next morning, it was to Dale knocking at his bedroom door. She leaned in and smiled, "Time to face the day, sleepy head. The day's a'wasting, besides Captain Dan is here to see you."

"Tell him I'll see him in my office in ten minutes."

Jumping from his bed, Doc quickly set about making himself presentable. Ten minutes later showered and dressed he entered his office. Shaking hands with Griffin he seated himself behind his desk. "Good morning Dan. What can I do for you this morning?"

Griffin smiled innocently at Doc, "Late night Miles?"

"Just work. House call on a client."

"Uh, huh. Didn't see your car outside. Car trouble?"

"It's in the shop, radiator trouble."

"Uh, huh. We had a busy night ourselves. It seems there was burglary at the Hilldale pharmacy last night. We had a car in the neighborhood and were in pursuit when things got hot."

"Really. What happened?"

"Well, one of the burglars had a machine gun. Made Swiss cheese out of our squad car. Fortunately both of my boys made it out with only minor injuries."

"That's good news about your men. Did the burglars get away?"

"Not exactly. Apparently someone else intervened. The getaway truck was shot up and crashed. One man dead, one in a coma at Memorial hospital and we think one more got away. No sign of the other car or its occupants, except for some auto glass, radiator water and skid marks."

"Do you think this has anything to do with the other drug thefts yesterday?"

"I'm certain of it. Since we broke up the inside theft ring these thugs have turned to open robbery to get what they want. Unfortunately that is rapidly turning the streets into a war zone. It's got to be stopped."

Doc nodded, "I'm doing everything I can. With a little luck I'll have something for you soon."

Griffin stood up and reached for his hat, "Take care of yourself, Miles. Call me if you need me."

When he had left, Dale came into the office, "I'm going home to rest for a while. I'll be back this afternoon. I checked the phone book and called information. Neither of those women are listed at all. I'll make some other checks this afternoon. My car is outside if you need it." As she breezed out the door, she smiled over her shoulder, "I hope you and Captain Dan had a nice chat." Before he could make a clever retort she was gone.

After Dale left, Doc checked on Tommy who seemed to be resting quietly. He then called his Down Street clinic to see how things were there and caught up with paperwork for an hour. When routine business seemed complete he went through into his surgery. He cleaned everything thoroughly and placed all his used instruments in the autoclave for sterilization. Finally, he carefully cleaned the slug he had taken out of Tommy's shoulder. Once clean he examined it under a magnifying glass. It was copper jacketed and in fairly good shape. Thoughtfully, he took a micrometer from a drawer of instruments and carefully measured the slug. The results were very interesting. He then looked in on Tommy who had recovered enough to eat some broth before falling back into a sound sleep.

Dale returned at three. She looked refreshed and reported that she had an idea about the women's names but had to make an additional phone call. Doc told her to use his office. Meanwhile he had things to do. Borrowing her keys, he left quietly though the back door.

Doc had taken the time to look up the address of the Zenith pharmacy and drove straight to it. Parking around the corner he went down the alley behind the shop. Quickly locating the back door, he pulled his Scar mask over his face and attempted to unlock the back door. The third key worked and the Scar turned the knob quietly, opening the door just far enough that he could hear what was going on inside. The only noise came from two voices speaking in the front of the store. Slipping inside he found himself in the back of the laboratory where the pharmacist obviously filled his client's prescriptions. Moving silently to the curtain that separated the store front from the rear, he peered through a narrow gap in it. A stocky middle-aged man in a white uniform was just bidding goodbye to an elderly woman. He turned toward the rear. Scar secreted himself next to the doorway and drew his pistol. The pharmacist, reading a prescription, was taken totally by surprise as he brushed through the curtain and found a revolver grinding into his ear.

"Don't make a sound," grated the hoarse voice into his ear. Scar then shoved the man hard in the back, he took two fast steps and slammed him nose first into the wall. Bouncing off, the Scar spun him around and again slammed him up against the wall. The light in the back room was rather dim but not so dim that the clearly terrified druggist didn't recognize his captor. "The Purple Scar!" he gasped.

"Correct, and you're George Russelli the crooked druggist."

The frightened druggist paled at these words, "I don't know what you're talking about mister."

"I think you do," hissed the twisted lips of the Scar. "I think you are selling morphine from your inventory on the black market because you're up to your neck in gambling debts. I also think you are part of the drug thefts from local hospitals and I think you know all about these drug hijackings going on around town."

Sweat sprang out on the druggist's face, "No, you got it wrong. I'm a victim. I was robbed yesterday."

Scar pressed the barrel of his revolver hard against the man's nose. "I don't believe you. I think I ought to just kill you and move on. I've killed so many men in the last few days one more won't matter." He thumbed back his gun's hammer with a loud double click. The druggist's legs began to fail him and he started to slide down the wall. The Scar used his free arm to support the terrified druggist's weight.

"No. Don't, please. I'll talk." Russelli, his courage gone went on to confess the truth. He was badly in debt. He had been selling his inventory off to drug addicts and street people. He had faked the robbery hoping to use the insurance money to cover his inventory losses. He continued to maintain his innocence of other robberies though. The Scar let him ramble through his confession and said nothing for some time afterward letting the man sweat his fate. Finally the Scar rasped out his verdict, "I'm leaving now. When I'm gone you will go immediately to police headquarters. You will ask for Captain Griffin. You will confess exactly what you have done and beg him to arrest you. Do you understand?"

The terrified Russelli gasped out, "Yes, yes I'll do it."

Leaning in until his hideous countenance was just inches away for the druggist The Scar hissed, "I have informants everywhere, including police headquarters. I'll know if you don't follow my instructions exactly. And if you don't, I will return here and burn this place down around you. Do you understand?"

The terrified druggist could only nod. The Scar forced him down to the floor and left quickly out the back door. Removing his mask, Doc drove quietly away. Driving to the main branch of the city library he parked and went inside. He went directly to the card catalog and sorted through several drawers. He made notations on the call numbers of several books and then went to the aisles to locate the designated volumes. He found what he was looking for in the third book, a world firearms reference. He joined the crowd leaving as it was nearly closing time. Once outside he made his plans as he drove back to Swank Street.

Dale was waiting for him. She told him Tommy was better and resting easily. Settled in his office with Dale, Doc asked her if she had found out about the women he had asked her to track down. She smiled and said, "Yes, I did and I think you'll be surprised." When she told him what she

"I will…burn this place down…"

had learned he was surprised. Thinking about it for a moment he said, "Dale, you've just given me the last piece of the puzzle. I believe I can find out who's behind this tonight but I'm going to need your help." He then told her of his plan.

At two o'clock the next morning Dale was behind the wheel of her coupe with Doc beside her. She drove quietly through the darkened city. They crossed downtown and headed for the docks. Doc directed her to turn down Front Street. To their right a row of warehouses separated them from the actual piers themselves. Over the warehouses they could see lights illuminating the piers. They passed a brighter group of lights illuminating a ship whose masts could be barely seen over a warehouse's roof. A block further on he had Dale pull over to the curb. He opened his door but did not step out. He turned to Dale, "You know what to do."She nodded. He continued, "40 minutes. If I haven't returned by then or you see the flare, I want you to leave. Drive to the clinic. Call Dan Griffin and tell him to bring every man he can. Then, I want you to stay with Tommy until I return. Don't leave the clinic, understand?"

It was dark in the car so Doc couldn't see she was biting her lip as she nodded. Slipping on his mask, he slipped a bulky flare gun into one pocket and started to get out of the coupe when Dale said, "Please be careful Darling."

He turned back to look at her. Dale did not see the horrible features of his mask; all she saw was the man she loved. Reaching out the forefinger of his right hand he gently touched the tip of her nose, "I always do." He then stepped out of the coupe and was swallowed up in the shadows.

The Scar moved down the dark side street between two dark warehouses toward the pier. Reaching the corner of the warehouse he peered carefully around the corner. To the left was an empty berth and shadows. Ahead, across fifty feet of empty pier was open water. The Scar could barely hear water lapping against the pilings over the noise from his right. There, perhaps a hundred yards away a ship was moored. The pier alongside it and the forward deck and side of the ship was bathed in light from floodlights on the ship's derrick and pier. Multiple large wooden crates on the pier were being loaded into nets. A net carrying a large crate was high in the air swinging over the ships side. A hesitation and then the whine of the derrick changed and the swaying crate was lowered toward the ship. Perhaps a dozen men were on the pier preparing the crates for loading. To the Scar's eye they all were dressed in longshoreman's clothing and seemed quite competent at their duties. Chances were they were all legitimate dock workers and not involved in the illegal business at hand but Scar couldn't be sure. His business was not with them anyway. He was more interested in who would be on the ship itself.

Waiting until he felt that no one on the pier was looking his way he dashed quietly across the pier and flattened himself on the rough wooden surface. Picking his way carefully along taking what cover he could find behind mooring bollards he made his way closer to the ship. Soon he was at the base of the heavy mooring rope that tied the stern to the dock. It was a good six inches in diameter and was tied around a heavy bollard and ran upwards at a fairly steep angle to the upper stern deck. Scar had come prepared and had on a pair of leather gloves. Leaning out he grasped the heavy line in both hands and letting go his feet he fell forward, his legs swinging free over the unseen water. Looping his legs upward he the wrapped them around the rope and began climbing upward. The heavy line sagged toward the water at first and then angled up even more steeply. It was very hard work and a lesser man would not have made it but the Scar worked out every day in the fully equipped gym at his residence and was in superb physical shape. Gritting his teeth under the flexible mask, the Scar struggled up the last few feet of rope until he could reach out and grab the edge of the steel deck. He rested there for a few moments while he looked and listened for movement on the darkened stern. Satisfied that no one was nearby Scar boosted himself over the rail and crouched down in the shadows. The stern was elevated above the main cargo deck. This deck stretched to the mid-ships' superstructure. Halfway along it, between the two raised cargo hatches was the aft derrick, a complicated structure of winches and booms. Everything forward of the superstructure was lit by bright lights while everything aft of it was thrown into deep shadows. The superstructure itself was dominated by the single large funnel. Wisps of smoke could be seen wafting from the funnel. This of course was why Scar could feel a gentle vibration through the soles of his feet from the huge engines.

Confident that every person aboard was either below decks or forward to help with the cargo loading, the Scar stepped briskly across the stern. Steep steps took him down to the main deck. Skirting the knee-high raised cargo hatches he strode to the superstructure and quickly located a closed hatch. Knocking loose the greased clips he cracked it and light flooded out on the aft deck. He listened but heard nothing. He then opened it enough to slip through, quickly closing it behind him and dogging the clips. He crept down a companion way with his revolver ready in his right hand, attempting to understand the layout of the cabins as he went. Some doors were plainly marked, others were not. The Scar knew the forward main deck would be crowded with men so he was looking for a stairwell down hoping to find an unseen way forward. He froze in place as he heard steps and whistling. Reaching for the nearest door handle he prayed silently that it be unlocked. It was and he pushed into a pitch black room closing the door quietly behind him. As he stood with his ear pressed to the door he became aware of slow heavy breathing behind him. He had stepped into the cabin of an off duty officer. He remained motionless and as soon as the whistling passed and faded, Scar slipped back into the corridor and continued.

Scar finally located a stair going down. Stepping off the stairs he rounded a corner and ran squarely into a man stepping into the corridor. Bouncing off the masked figure the crewman started an angry comment but his mouth instead dropped open as he went pale, stunned by the horrific figure before him. He never got the chance to recover because the Scar's left hook caught him on the point of his jaw and he staggered back against the wall and fell to the corridor deck unconscious. Holstering his gun, Scar grabbed the unconscious man by the heels and dragged him into the cabin he had just left. It took perhaps three minutes to tie him hand and foot and gag him using bed sheets torn from the bunk.

Leaving the cabin the Purple Scar quickly located another stairway and dropped down another deck. This deck was not paneled. Metal pipes ran overhead. Orienting himself Scar moved forward, opening every hatch and door he came to, searching for a way forward. Eventually he opened a hatch revealing a short corridor and another hatch. The second hatch, when opened, revealed shadowy darkness and raucous noise. Noticing a light switch next to the hatch Scar pressed it and plunged the corridor into darkness. Opening the forward hatch fully he realized he was in the hold. A metal wall ran forward on his left. To his right were stacks of wooden crates stacked higher than his head. Above him he could see the glare of lights and a confused mix of voices, shouts and heavy machinery noise. He was in deep shadow and could see no one.

Moving cautiously ahead down the narrow aisle between the wall and row of crates he was all but invisible to any one unless they were atop a crate and looking directly down on him. He made no noise that could be heard above the din of crates being lowered into the hold. Reaching the forward wall of the hold he came to another closed hatch. Turning the clips that held it shut he pulled it open. It squeaked loudly but the noise was swallowed up amidst the background noise. The next compartment was in total darkness. Stepping through, the Scar closed the hatch behind him. Taking out his pencil flashlight he turned it on to find that he was in another aisle sandwiched between a wall and stacks of crates. Without doubt he was in the most forward hold. Flashing the light overhead he could see the large hatch cover was closed. He moved all the way to the forward corner of the hold. Another hatch led forward but more interestingly there were welded rungs set into the wall leading upward. With his pen light he glanced at his watch, fifteen minutes to the deadline he had given Dale. He hoped she would do as he asked and not try anything foolish.

Pocketing both the pen light and gun he climbed the ladder. At the top was a metal hatch perhaps three feet square. He grasped the handle and turned. The hatch opened silently, letting in all the outside noise. Opening the hatch a little further the Purple Scar raised his head above the edge and looked around. He was at the forward port corner of the forward hold. Aft, across the forward hold cover was the open second hold. Between the two stood the derrick assembly with its massive cable drum, motor and winch controls. A man was working the controls as he watched. Other men lined the edge of the open hatch and from the sound of it there were more men down in the hold itself, probably standing atop the already loaded crates.

Crawling out on to the hold cover he let the hatch drop silently behind him and he began crawling slowly across the hold cover toward the derrick assembly. The bright searchlights mounted on the derrick pointed down at the open hold, so the area behind the derrick he was crawling through was in deep shadow. Ten feet from the winch operator's back he took stock. A lot of men were moving about and yelling but he finally saw the man he had come for. He was over to the port side of the open hold about fifty feet away. There, a tall man was pointing and yelling orders and people seemed to be paying attention to him; the leader, the man behind all this. Unfortunately, he was wearing a wide brimmed hat and a long trench coat and the Scar could not see his face. No matter though, he was here and that's what counted. Scar knew he had to capture the man or failing that he had to keep him here for the police. Drawing his revolver he rose to one knee and lunged toward the winch operator.

The operator never knew what hit him. Scar's revolver came down hard on the top of his head. He grunted and collapsed in a heap. Scar stood up next to the controls. He could see more now. A crate was suspended twenty feet over the hold ready to be lowered. Men stood atop crates in the hold ready to receive it. Perfect. Scar reached into his left pocket and removed the bulky form of the flare gun. He broke it open and loaded it with a large flare. Snapping it closed he thumbed back the hammer and raised it over his head. As his arm was going up past about sixty degrees he was struck by something heavy and moving fast. His finger involuntarily squeezed the trigger and a blindingly bright red flare shot into the sky as the Purple Scar crashed to the deck under the weight of an attacker. Catlike the Scar squirmed from under his attacker punching and kicking. They both reached their feet at the same time. His hulking enemy aimed a roundhouse punch at his head but the Scar ducked underneath it and answered with a right-left-right combination. The man grunted and was going to punch again when a flurry of bullets rained around the combatants. Scar dove to the deck. His opponent, not so lucky clutched his chest and sank to the deck beside him.

Chaos reigned as the Scar quickly looked around. Several men had pulled guns and were shooting in his direction. The leader had crouched down but was till shouting as he pointed at the Scar's concealed position. Most interesting, high above the deck, the suspended crate was burning like a torch. Apparently the flare, instead of going high into the air overhead had made a direct hit on the crate swaying above the hold. Whatever was inside was even more flammable than the wooden crate itself and it was a now a large fireball. Scar decided this suited him just fine. He reached forward and started shoving levers around. One of them must have been the cable brake because the drum suddenly began turning and the burning crate crashed down into the hold amidst screams of warning. Regaining his revolver the Scar triggered two shots toward the starboard side of the hold and two toward the portside to keep people's heads down. He then ducked down to reload.

Reloaded he crawled toward the port side keeping below the level of the hatch cover. Bullets flew overhead some striking various bits of metal and ricocheting around the ship, some burying themselves in the wooden hatch cover or winch station. The grim masked avenger reached the port edge of the hatch and risked a look around it. Two men had closed the distance and were just fifteen feet away. They saw him immediately and fired as he did. Bullets crossed in mid-air. The first man took a slug in the chest and spun out of sight. The other ducked down but yelled at the top of his lungs, "God, it's the Purple Scar!"

Reloading again, the Scar peered over the edge of the hold and saw the leader had turned and was running aft yelling as he went. Bracing his revolver on the edge of the hold with both hands, he fired at the fleeing man. Blam! Blam! Blam! The range was long and the light poor but on his third shot he saw the leader lurch and grab his arm. Scar fired again but the leader disappeared into a hatch in the superstructure. He reloaded his gun with his last four rounds and retreated forward along the high rail firing as he went. Bullets flew but his luck held and he wasn't hit. He finally took cover behind a metal mount of some kind near the raised foredeck. Gunshots fired his way had decreased, probably because most people were now more concerned by the huge flames leaping up out of the open hold. Every bit of the forward part of the ship was lit up bright as day. The flare hadn't worked as he intended but the Scar reckoned that this little blaze more than made up for it.

Men were running everywhere but mainly toward the gangway and down to the pier. This made the alternative quite attractive. Holstering his revolver Scar took off his jacket and threw it over the side of the ship, his shoes followed. He quickly climbed to the railing and without a look back he dove over the side. In his alter ego the Scar had earned college letters in swimming and had picked up more than a little about diving as well. His classic swan dive was seen by no one in the dark but was still a thing of beauty. He entered the water cleanly with very little splash. He went deep but swam strongly for the surface. He surfaced and gulped air. Treading water and looking about his view was dominated by the pillar of fire coming from the forward hold of the freighter. He turned and stroked strongly toward the stern. As he swam past it he glanced up at the name painted across the rounded stern. There wasn't much light but just enough that he could make out the name. *Andrea Toroni* was painted in large letters on the rounded stern.When he was a couple of hundred yards past the freighter he angled toward the pier and found a ladder to climb dripping out onto the dock. He could hear sirens so he turned away from the burning ship into the darkness. As he slipped away he removed his mask and tossed it into the dark water. He could always make another.

Sometime later Doc was making his way from building to building attempting to a stay in the shadows as he worked his way away from the docks. He took cover whenever a police car or fire truck went by because he was quite a sight; soaking wet, no coat, no shoes and his holstered revolver prominent on his hip. He ducked into a doorway as headlights turned a corner toward him. A car drove slowly down the street and as it neared Doc recognized it. He stepped out into the street as Dale braked her coupe to a stop. Leaning out the window she looked him up and down. "Need a ride mister?" she smilingly inquired.

Doc opened the door and collapsed on the seat, "Yes, I could sure use one."

Glancing over her shoulder Dale said, "I see you've been busy." Doc could only nod.

Much later that night Doc Murdock managed to get hold of Captain Griffin. He gave him a bare bones version of the battle on the freighter and told him he needed to make a special arrest, "I'm sure there will be plenty of proof once we can sort through the records but the important thing is he'll have a bullet wound in his left arm. I put it there myself and I hope it hurts like the devil after all the trouble he's caused this town." Griffin agreed and they made plans to meet downtown at headquarters the next day.

Late the next morning Miles Murdock was dressed and ready to face the day. Tommy was much improved and Dale had firm instructions to keep him from attempting to do too much. Again borrowing Dale's coupe he drove downtown and found a parking place close to Police headquarters. Once at the main desk he asked for Captain Griffin and was told he was out but was expected momentarily.

Just as he was taking a seat on the waiting bench there was a flurry of activity at the main entrance. Standing up, Doc could see that several squad cars had pulled up out front and officers were pulling handcuffed men out of them. Doc watched with secret pleasure as police officers marched handcuffed men past him. Some were dressed in sailor's clothing, others in working clothes and several were in cheap suits. Captain Dan Griffin personally marched the final culprit through the main doors his hands cuffed in front of him. They stopped in front of Doc and Griffin spoke up loudly, "Good morning Doctor Murdock. You've met Mr. Kline here haven't you? It looks like he's been the gentleman responsible for all these stolen drugs lately. Excuse me while I see to his comfort."

Doc smiled, "Take your time captain, I'm in no hurry."

Later, seated in Griffin's office they compared notes. Griffin related the arrests made at the Acme plant. Kline had not put up a fight but refused to say anything. Griffin shook his head. "He doesn't have to talk. We have enough to hang him several times over. It seems his real name was Klein. His parents are ethnic Germans who live in Milwaukie. They came over before the last war when Kline was just a boy. He Americanized his name but always harbored strong feelings for Germany, a closet Nazi I guess. He was hijacking his own products for shipment to Europe. To cover all the extra raw materials he was using he started the pilfering ring, more drugs to go out by ship and extra orders from the hospitals and pharmacies to justify his extra production. The home office had no clue as to what was going on. But how did you get onto them Miles?"

Doc smiled, "Kline was one of my suspects, along with Russelli the pharmacist and a doctor at City hospital for a while but I really began to lean toward Kline after the shootout with his hijackers. One of them was using a strange submachine gun I had never seen before. It fired 9mm slugs, not an American caliber. Some research revealed it was a 1928 Bergman made in Germany. I was sure that no doctor or druggist would have access to exotic weaponry like that. The final straw was Dale figuring out that the women's names I found written in Kline's calendar were actually the names of freighters. With the *Toroni* sailing at dawn this morning I knew that the mastermind behind all this would be on board to supervise the shipment. I wanted to capture him for you if possible, but things sort of got out of hand."

Griffin waved a hand, "Fortunately Dale didn't wait for your signal but had us on the way early. The fire department got there in plenty of time, the ship was never in danger. Although a lot of important drugs were burned up. That reminds me, last night the druggist Russelli marched in here and demanded to be arrested. He confessed to faking his robbery and selling illegal drugs to street addicts. He seemed quite relieved to be behind bars. You wouldn't know anything about that, would you?"

Doc smiled, "I'm glad to see that Russelli had an attack of conscience. It helps restore my belief in my fellow man. As for some of the drugs being destroyed, that was an accident. But at least they didn't end up in the hands of Fascists overseas." He then smiled, "And Acme certainly has the capacity to make more, now don't they?" Griffin barked out a short laugh. As Doctor Murdock got up to leave he asked, "Where are you off to now?" Doc, his hand on the door knob turned back, "I've got to see about getting my car fixed, and check on Tommy. Then I'm going to go home and rest. It's been a long week.

THE END

PURPLE PROSE FOR THE PURPLE SCAR

I love the pulps, all of them: Westerns, Detectives, Flying Adventures, Jungle Adventures, everything. But my favorites and perhaps the most popular of all the pulps were the Masked Avengers. Even today many of the most easily remembered heroes of the pulp era are characters like The Shadow, The Spider, Moon Man, Green Lama. Their exotic names, frightening appearance and secret identities thrilled readers then and still do. Since the Masked Avenger characters were always my favorites you can imagine how excited I was when Ron Fortier gave me a chance to write a story about one of them. Granted, the hero chosen was one of the lesser known ones but a Masked Vigilante is still a Masked Vigilante and I was excited I'd get to write about one them.

First a word about The Purple Scar. Wait, the Purple Scar? Never heard of him you say? Perhaps that's because the Purple Scar appeared in only four issues of Exciting Detective magazine in 1941-42. He was a classic masked avenger who wore a mask modeled on his murdered brother's death features who was a respected plastic surgeon in his spare time; a tried and true formula. Unfortunately, he appeared at a time when the public's tastes were changing. The exotic masked heroes were fading while detective stories were on the rise. Is that why the Purple Scar only lasted four issues? Perhaps, maybe it was cutbacks caused by America gearing up to fight a war. I don't know, but I believe the Purple Scar had a lot of unrealized potential. It's too bad he got only four issues, with more time to develop or perhaps a different writer he might have been one of the more remembered Masked Heroes. He had a cool name and wore a horrific fright mask with which to terrify the underworld. Unfortunately, the stories weren't written as action adventures. They were pretty much drawing room mysteries with our hero running around collecting clues, establishing suspects and unmasking the villain at the end. A well tested formula for a rich amateur detective but a real disappointment when compared to The Shadow or The Spider who preferred to deal out justice with the barrels of their automatics.

I set out to make the Scar's new adventures what I think they could have been with a little more imagination. I wanted to make his adventures faster paced and more exciting. I decided what was needed was more sneaking around terrifying the underworld and fewer speeches to assembled suspects so I styled his adventure as if he was one of the classic masked heroes from the early thirties. I wanted to let him use the full potential of his frightening appearance without losing all the flavor of the character as written in Exciting Detective. I believe it came out pretty well. The plot wasn't hard to come up with. It was inspired by the heroes' profession and the time frame of the story and it came together fairly easily. No diabolical plots endangering humanity, just good old fashioned criminals that need to be stopped by our hero.

Writing a detective story, even a pulp detective story, is harder than writing horror or pure adventure, especially a "who dunnit mystery." As a writer everything has to mesh, you have to have plausible culprits and lots of clues. Everything has to come out just right at the end, so the reader will say to himself "Ah, I thought it might be him." The clues are the worst part. Make them too simple and your readers will figure out the end too early in the story. Make them too hard and your readers lose interest or are incredulous, "That came out of left field. How could *he* have done it?" It's a fine line and sometimes takes a good bit of thought. I guess we'll just have to see if I kept close enough to that line to keep people interested.

In the end, writing *Liquid Death* took a bit more work than the Ravenwood adventure *Heart of Darkness* I recently completed but it was just as satisfying. The Purple Scar turned out to be a lot of fun. I don't think I've added him to the royalty of Masked Vigilantes but I hope this adventure is a good reminder of those fast paced, exciting stories of the Masked Heroes that readers loved. Fun, that's what reading the pulps was all about, fun. If you have fun reading *Liquid Death* then I succeeded. I sure had a lot of fun writing it.

GENE MOYERS -studied European and Medieval history at the University of Oregon. He is a former U.S. Army armor crewman. He worked in the High Tech industry for some time and ran a store front and internet hobby shop for several years. An avid military gamer and role player his favorite game was *Daredevils* set in the 1930s. His love affair with the 1930s and pulps in particular stem from his first time reading a *Shadow* novel as a boy. Although interested in writing since a teen he did not turn to serious writing until 2000. He is the co-author of *GURPS Crusades* published by Steve Jackson Games and has written a Ravenwood adventure for the second volume of that series. When not working on Airship 27 projects he is busy writing horror adventures for his swashbuckling character set in Colonial America. Gene currently lives in Beaverton Oregon with his wife and three lazy dogs.

THE MURDER SYNDICATE
BY GARY LOVISI

Albert Alsace was feeling quite full of himself as he walked down the streets of Akelton City that cool autumn evening. He was a lawyer with the large and powerful Stepford Corporation and had closed the deal of his career on a merger that would net him a hefty sum in the stock market. He smiled to himself as he walked to his apartment house on prestigious Swank Street—as nice as those accommodations were, once his ship came in with the profit from this merger, he knew he'd become an instant millionaire. Life just didn't get much sweeter! Then it was a palatial estate and a horse farm in the country for him. But he knew he had to keep his unlawful shenanigans under wraps until the moment of the merger. He'd already purchased tens of thousands of dollars of devalued Stepford stock, now he just wanted to go home and wait to collect his money once the value shot through the roof. In the meantime he just hoped no one knew about what he had done.

Albert Alsace nodded to Herbert his doorman at the ritzy building in which his apartment was located. It had been a long day and he was tired and needed a drink. As he waited for the elevator to take him to his 10th Floor apartment, a lovely young woman came by and stood next to him also obviously waiting for the car to arrive. There were two elevators but as yet none had arrived. Alsace took another look at the lovely woman beside him and realized that he was not all in that much of a hurry to get home.

"Good evening," Alsace said in a friendly manner, turning on the charm with a warm smile. The woman was certainly attractive and he saw no wedding ring on her finger.

"Oh, hello," she replied with a short grin as if she had just noticed him.

"You must be a new tenant here, or perhaps you are just visiting?" he asked, knowing he was being a bit forward but he was too curious about her to let it go. She seemed friendly enough too.

She allowed a little smile, "Oh, just visiting. Actually, it's business. My name is Dorothy Vane."

The man was charmed and he held out his hand, "And my name is Albert. Albert Alsace."

She took his hand and shook it warmly, "Nice to meet you, Albert."

"Likewise, Dorothy."

She looked at him closely and nodded, apparently liking what she saw, "Oh, here's our car. Let's ride up together."

The arrows of the dial above settled on the "L" and then the elevator doors opened onto the lobby. The elevator was empty and there was no one else in the lobby at the moment. Albert couldn't believe his good fortune. He would be alone with this most striking woman and perhaps even be able to spark a friendship with her and...

"After you," he said, gallantly allowing her to enter the elevator car first.

"Oh, and a gentleman too! Thank you," she replied as she walked inside and he followed her. The doors closed and the elevator slowly moved upwards. He only just remembered to press the "ten" button for his floor.

"Oh, you are going to the tenth?" Dorothy asked him as she began to rummage in her purse for something. She looked up at him, "I can never find anything I need in here, pardon me."

He nodded with an indulgent grin, how any woman could ever find anything in such a large purse never ceased to amazed him. Why did they carry so much...junk? Albert smiled, deciding to be bold, "Yes, it certainly is a big purse you have there. You know, I have an apartment on the tenth. I'm in 10A. It's quite nice. Perhaps when you are finished with your business you'd consider dropping in for a drink?"

"That's such a coincidence because my business takes me to the Tenth Floor."

"Really?" Alsace asked curiously now.

"Yes," Dorothy replied, then she withdrew her hand from her purse and at the end of it was a cold steel grey .38 which she pointed at the startled man before her.

"Dorothy, what's this...?" Alsace stammered in shock.

"Sorry, Albert, but business is business," then the young woman pressed the trigger and sent four slugs into Albert Alsace's chest. He fell to the floor in a bloody heap, his dreams of impending wealth soon as dead as he was.

The woman who called herself Dorothy Vane put the .38 back into her purse and quickly hit every button in the car from the Eleventh to Twentieth Floors. Then she got out of the elevator on the Tenth Floor when the doors opened, quickly entering the elevator next over, down to the lobby and out of the building.

+++

One week later Martin Smith was enjoying a quiet evening at the Bistro on Fourth Street with the woman he loved. She was not his wife. However, Martin was hoping that someday soon she would be, once the impediment to that happy event was once and for all out of his way. That impediment being Cathy, his wife of ten years.

"Have another drink, my love," Martin told the lovely young woman next to him at the dinner table. The Bistro was a cozy place and Martin and Samantha were close together and drinking rather too much but enjoying it nevertheless. Martin kissed the young woman feverishly, hungrily, and she returned his hot kisses with a passion equally felt.

"Oh, Martin, I've missed you the last few days," Samantha whispered in a dusky voice as she drew him closer to her. They were rather making a scene with their intense embraces but neither of them cared.

"I had some things to settle. They are being worked on right now. In fact, I'm waiting on a phone call at eight o'clock that should settle everything once and for all," he told her as he took another drink.

Samantha broke off their embrace, looked at the gold wristwatch he had given her for her birthday and said, "Well, it's almost eight now, darling."

"Oh, right!" he said giving her a kiss as he got up from the table. "Don't go away, doll. I'll make that call now and then be right back."

Martin Smith hummed a popular tune as he walked to the back of the restaurant and sat down in a phone booth, closing the door behind him. He picked up the phone, put coins in the box and then dialed the special number, waiting for the coded message.

The phone dialed and then rang at the other end. It was picked up and a man's voice said, "Yes?"

Martin Smith took a deep breath, he had contracted out for the murder of his wife, Cathy, with these people. The "job" was supposed to be done before eight o'clock this evening. Now he had to place the call for verification. It was a nerve-wracking situation, this murder of his wife of so many years but there was no other alternative because Cathy stood in the way of his being with his beloved Samantha—and nothing—no one—could be allowed to come between Martin and the woman he wanted.

"Yes?" the voice at the other end of the line repeated.

Martin Smith grew nervous. This was it! This was the message he had been waiting for, the coded message that would tell him that Cathy was dead, the victim of a robbery gone bad at their home while he had been absent. It had all been planed perfectly. He sighed deeply, then collect his thoughts.

"I'm calling about that job," he asked nervously, using the prearranged code, anticipation building within him. He wanted to get his message and be gone, for even now there was someone outside his booth waiting to use the phone. In fact, he noticed with a sly grin, that it was a most attractive young woman. He smiled at her, motioning that he'd just be one minute longer, and she smiled back patiently.

Smith waited for the response from the man on the phone.

It was not what he expected.

"There was a problem," the voice at the other end of the line spoke rather matter-of-factly, and a sudden icy chill ran down Smith's spine and sweat broke out on his forehead. This was not the proper response at all!

"What do you mean a problem?" Smith asked in growing apprehension.

"We had a counter offer," the voice told him coldly.

"A...counter offer...?"

"Yes...and we took it," the voice spoke in dire warning as the phone at the other end was suddenly hung up.

Martin Smith stood frozen in astonishment and terror, starring at the phone and trying to comprehend what he had just been told. Could it be true? What did it mean? He was shocked, frozen in deep thought when his attention was drawn by a couple of light taps to the glass door of the telephone booth he was in. He suddenly grew angry, it had to be that woman waiting to make her call. He looked over at her with an angry glance, annoyed and then shocked to see she was holding a gun pointed right at his chest.

"What?" he asked in a shrill voice. "No!"

The gun went off and three slugs entered Martin Smith's chest and stopped his heart. He was dead right away and the attractive young woman who had shot him dead quickly escaped through the back door of the restaurant and was never seen again.

+++

Doctor Miles Murdock was in the laboratory of his office on Swank Street busy working on a secret compound for use in the new mask for the man he liked to call his alter ego. As a respected surgeon who specialized in plastic surgery, Murdock was world renowned in his profession, but he had a secret side to his life, a much darker side. He was also the ace crime fighting masked avenger, the Purple Scar!

Murdock mixed the various solutions together to form the new compound that he would pour into the mold to make his mask. The mask was made of pliable rubber. This latest mask included a new element to the mix, glowing phosphorous colors, most notably a dark purple that would give the face of the mask an even more sinister effect. That was Murdock's purpose, to match the effect in his mask of that look he had seen upon his dead brother's face years ago. Miles Murdock's older brother, John, had been a heroic city policeman who had been murdered by gunmen. However, the killers had not just murdered Miles, they had destroyed his handsome face by throwing acid on it and then dumped his body into the river. When John's body had been found ten days later, Captain Dan Griffin of the Akelton City Police Department's Homicide Squad had called in Miles to identify his brother's body.

Miles had been devastated by what he had seen, for not only had his beloved brother been murdered, but the mutilation of John's face by acid was incomprehensible. Simply evil. Seeing what had been done to John did something to the young doctor, it surely enraged him, but it also fired him with a fierce determination to fight crime and find the man who was the brains behind his brother's horrendous killing.

However, the most shocking aspect of the entire crime was the stark image that remained forever burned into the mind of young Miles Murdock to this day—the appearance of his brother's face. After being doused with acid and soaked in the river waters for ten days what presented itself to him was the face of a terrible dead rotting corpse. John's flesh had been eaten away by the acid and submerged in water that had caused it to turn a dark purple. It looked terrible and terrifying and it was then that Miles knew he would make a mask of that face to mirror his dead brother's features in his own fight against crime. A purple mask. Composed of dreadful scars. Purple becomes black at night, which would make his face nearly invisible instead of betraying it by a pale glow in the darkness. Thus, Doctor Miles Murdock became, the Purple Scar.

Now Murdock was working on completing his latest project, an upgrade to his scar mask using phosphorescent colors with a particularly striking phosphorescent purple dye mixed into the rubber compound. Now he would pour that compound into the mold to make a much thinner but more strong and pliant rubber mask. It was almost ready. He withdrew the new mask from the mold and gingerly placed it into a box that held a manikin head and small electric fans on all sides. He placed the mask upon the head of the manikin and turned on the fans. The head spun slowly, while the fans in the box blew a gentle swirl of cool air to speed in the drying of the rubber.

"This looks like the best one yet," Murdock said to himself as his eyes feasted on the grimly terrifying visage of the Purple Scar mask. Murdock nodded grimly, "It even scares me!"

Once the mask was dry and ready Murdock carefully took it off the display head and took a closer look at it. It was surely a grim piece of work, dark and bizarrely terrifying, looking exactly like his brother John's face had appeared when they had pulled his dead body out of the river. It was soft, pliant rubber. Murdock found that he could easily ball it up in one hand, his fist completely covering the thing, then open his hand and the mask was ready to wear.

Murdock tried on the new mask. It fit perfectly. Then he turned off the lights. The room was in total darkness, but the phosphorous particles embedded in the rubber of the mask had absorbed enough light so they now gave off an eerie glow that resembled death itself. It was ghastly.

Suddenly the door to his lab burst open and Tommy Pedlar quickly walked into the room, "Hey, Boss, you okay? I saw the lights go out and --- whoa! What's that! My God...it's...hideous!"

"The new mask, Tommy. You like it?"

"'Like' ain't the proper word, Boss. It's something out of this world when you see it in the dark like this. It's a nightmare mask."

"Good, then it should work well instilling terror into criminals when they are forced to confront the Purple Scar in the dark of night."

"I'll say!"

"Turn on the lights, Tommy, this experiment has been a success," Murdock stated.

"So that's the new Scar face then?"

"Yes," Murdock replied as he took the mask off his head and placed it into his laboratory safe. Murdock always kept the mask in a safe when he was between cases like he was now. When on a case, he had a secret pocket that was sewn into his coat to hide it. This newer mask was much more pliant than the previous one, which had been damaged in a fight weeks ago. This one could be more easily balled up into his fist, it fit in the palm of his hand, so it would be just a tiny mass easy to hide on his person—but also easy to tuck away in his secret pocket always within reach for him to transform into The Purple Scar.

"That's an even scarier Scar mask than the other one, Boss," Tommy added in awe. Tommy was devoted to Miles Murdock. Tommy Pedlar was one of only three people in the world who knew Murdock's secret. He had been a street-wise hood known as "The Sticky-fingers Kid"—a very slick, former second story man. Murdock had saved Tommy's daughter's life and as a result the thief had become the Purple Scar's most trusted agent. The two were fast friends.

There were two other people who knew the secret identity of the Scar. One was Captain Dan Griffin of the Akelton Police Homicide Squad. This square-jawed, square-shouldered tough cop had a rock-hard lined face and black eyes. He had known both John and Miles for years and knew what Miles was doing in his one-man war against crime as the Purple Scar. He watched his friend's actions with curiosity and some awe. Griffin was not keen on vigilantism but he knew that sometimes it could be useful when fighting crime to have someone who could go where the cops could not—and do things in ways that the cops were not allowed to do.

The third person who knew the secret identity of the Purple Scar was the woman who loved the man behind the tortured mask. That woman was the lovely Dale Jordan. Dale was a chief nurse and had been with Miles for years. When she offered to help him find those responsible for his brother's murder, he accepted. She was tall, gracefully slender, with long-lashed emerald eyes and a soft, musical voice. The twenty-two year-old beauty was clearly in love with Murdock, and he with her, but his prime mission for now was to find the men who had murdered his brother. Murdock was always apprehensive about getting Dale involved in his crime-fighting cases because he feared for her safety, but he knew she was someone he could always count on. Her enthusiasm was just as great as his own to fight crime.

Miles Murdock put the new mask away in the lab safe, closed the door and walked over to Tommy. "It's been quiet lately round town. You notice that?"

"Yeah, you think the criminals all went on vacation?"

"Hardly," Murdock laughed, "but something's brewing. I can feel it."

"Boss, when it's quiet like this and it seems like nothing is going on, I think that's when you really gotta worry," Tommy advised.

"Well spoken. I think you're right. In fact, there have been a couple of unusual murders the last few weeks that have piqued my interest," Murdock stated.

"Yeah, I heard all about them, Boss. That ritzy lawyer Alsace was shot in an elevator. You know he had an apartment in a fancy building right down the block here on Swank Street?"

"Yes, I am aware of that," Murdock replied thoughtfully.

"Oh, well, of course," Tommy answered, nodding, for he knew his boss was aware of all the major criminal acts in the city. "Then there was that guy in the Bistro restaurant, shot to death in a phone booth while he was making a call. Now that ain't right. Poor guy can't even have a private moment on the phone without getting a chest full of slugs."

"The newspapers say no one has been arrested for either murder," Murdock stated dryly.

"Yeah, no one can figure it. What do the cops tell you? Did you speak about it to Captain Griffin yet?"

"Yes, he seems to think that there is some mysterious women behind it somehow."

"A woman? You mean a woman killer?"

"Yes, Tommy."

"Wow!"

The man at the other end of the table spoke in a low voice but with a power that put fear into the man seated at the other end of the table. "You have to understand that what some lowly newspaper reporter has dubbed 'The Murder Syndicate'—a rather crude but ample description of our work for lack of a better phrase — makes its services available to anyone in need. Anyone who can pay, that is. Anyone at all. I prefer to use the term 'Conspiracy of Silence,' because those who use our services enter into a partnership with us. You see, they can never speak of what they know without themselves showing equal guilt. You understand?'

"Yes," came the halting reply.

"Now we contract out jobs for any person willing to pay to have themselves—shall we say, relieved of another person's annoying or troublesome existence. Our services include jobs done for lawyers, businessmen, store owners, ex-wives, cheating husbands, doctors, politicians, even the police. And of course, jobs done *to* these people, as well. It is a growth industry here in Akelton City, and I have a small professional and very dedicated staff to assist me in this work."

The man at the other end of the table gulped nervously and then nodded his head in assent.

"Good. Now, Mr. Mayor, how can I be of assistance to you?"

✝✝✝

Five days later at the Carson Campaign Headquarters the buzz was in the air. The reform mayoral candidate for Akelton City had pulled ahead in the newspaper polls and the scent of victory was in the air. None felt it more deeply than Adele Carson herself, who was applauded by the staff of the office in a resounding crescendo of approval. Lately the candidate had noticed a lot of new faces in the office, young men and women for whom the reform message had real meaning and it brought a smile to the candidate's face. One of those newcomers was a hard-working young woman who had begun only yesterday. She showed a strong work ethic and endless zeal as if she were on a mission herself. Carson was especially happy to see that young women such as this one had been attracted to her campaign.

"You have an interview with Simmons of *The Chronicle* in ten minutes," one of the aides informed Carson quickly.

"All right, I'll be ready, I just have to make a quick stop in the ladies room to check my make-up," Carson replied with a girlish smile.

In the woman's restroom, Adele Carson, lawyer and widow of wealthy industrialist Ted Carson, checked her make-up in the mirror. Being a woman and running for office during this modern decade of the 1930s seemed to some a novelty, but Adele Carson was deadly serious with her reform agenda. She was certainly something new in politics. Women had only received the right to vote less than ten years earlier and she well remembered the struggle to achieve that right.

Now Adele Carson felt she was not only a serious candidate but a role model to young women everywhere. It was a mighty challenge for her to uphold—but she knew her brand of reform was dearly needed in corrupt Akelton City with the current mayor who had to be voted out of office. She reapplied her make-up as the door opened and a young woman entered the restroom. It was that same young women she had noticed who had begun working yesterday with the campaign.

"Oh, hello," the young woman said with a smile. "Should I leave? You look busy?"

"Not at all," Adele Carson told her with an indulgent grin. "Just doing a few touch ups before I meet with the press."

"Well, Mrs. Carson, I just wanted to say..." the young woman halted, obviously having become emotional for a moment, then continued, "I just wanted to say that I am so proud of what you are doing. You know, being a woman and all...?"

"Why, thank you, young lady," Carson said, more concerned at that moment with her looks reflected to her in the mirror than the woman before her, but not untouched by the young woman's remarks. "What is your name?"

"My name?" the young woman giggled girlishly, as though it were an honor for the candidate to even ask her the question. "That hardly matters."

"Of course it does, my dear. Now what is your name?"

"Dorothy."

"Dorothy, that is a lovely name. Dorothy what?"

Dorothy smiled sweetly ignoring the question and replied, "I think I have something here in my purse that may help you with the touch up."

"Really? Well I hope so, this make-up is just not working for me today," Carson replied, shaking her head as she looked at her face in the mirror critically.

Dorothy rummaged in her purse and pulled out something. What it was, was a steel grey .38 which she pointed right at the candidate. "Here it is, Mrs. Carson."

Adele Carson turned and looked at the young woman in utter surprise, "Is this some sort of joke?"

"No, and I am sorry. I really respect you for what you are doing—you have an important job to do cleaning up this city—but I also have my own job to do…"

Then Dorothy pulled the trigger three times and Adele Carson slipped to the floor dead.

+++

Tommy Pedlar brought in the news blasted all over the front page of *The Chronicle*. In a big blaring headline it told "Mayoral Candidate Adele Carson Murdered!" Then below the fold more headlines proclaimed, "Reform Ticket in Jeopardy!"

"Boss, you're not going to like this," Tommy said handing the papers to Miles Murdock who perused them with grim despair. He had known Adele Carson and her husband well and liked both of them.

"She was the one bright hope for our city, Tommy, now she is gone," Murdock said tersely, barely able to hold back his rage. "These killers have gone too far!"

"But how do we catch them? No one knows where to look, Boss," Tommy answered.

Murdock nodded, scanning the front page, where he noticed a particular interesting article below the fold near the lower corner. It was small, barely a one-inch column but it proclaimed "Murder Syndicate Runs Rampant".

"These killers have gone too far!"

The article blasted police and the city administration and spoke about a murder-for-hire group operating in Akelton City.

"This is interesting," Murdock stated. "Have you ever heard of this reporter, Byron James, Tommy?"

"Nope. Must be some new guy."

"Maybe some new young guy hungry for a good story and to make a name for himself. He seems to think all these recent murders are connected and I'm inclined to agree. He posits a murder for hire ring."

"I don't know about that, Boss, but I guess anything is possible."

"In this town it certainly is, Tommy. I think I will visit this Byron James, but first I want to see Dan and find out what the police are doing about this."

Miles Murdock brushed back his curly black hair, put on his dark coat and then left the office and headed to his shiny black sedan. The vehicle started up right away and purred like a kitten as he drove it down the street to police headquarters.

+++

When he got to the floor where the Homicide Squad was stationed he was ushered in to Captain Dan Griffin's office immediately by the secretary.

"Griff," Murdock said as the two friends shook hands, "good to see you."

"Miles, I knew you'd be here soon once the news hit the papers about the murder of Carson."

"Yes, a great tragedy. Any suspects? Witnesses?"

"No suspects," Griffin replied grimly, "but we're working on it hard. One of the campaign staffers remembered a young woman walking towards the restroom about the same time Carson had gone there. She had an appointment with a newspaper reporter and left to fix her make-up. She was only gone for a minute, then she was shot to death in the restroom."

Miles Murdock sighed deeply. "A real shame."

"I know," Griffin replied sadly.

"What are you doing about it?" Murdock asked his friend.

"Everything we can. We're turning the city upside down but nothing solid has come up. We're looking for this young woman, of course, but as yet no dice. She uses a .38, but that's about all we know. I am sure she's been wearing different disguises, using different wigs. At least the few witnesses we have on recent murders report a woman with different color hair and hair of different lengths. In one case she was a blonde with long locks, in another she had short bobbed black hair. In another case she wore a hat, in another she didn't wear a hat; wore glasses, didn't wear glasses. You get the story."

"A pro hitter," Murdock stated simply.

"Yes, I think so."

"And a woman. That is unusual."

Griffin nodded, "That's what makes it so difficult. Not only the fact that she's a woman, but she's so darn good at what she does. She gets in quick, does the job, then seems to disappear."

"What about the murder of Carson at her campaign headquarters? The killer had to sign up, identify herself if she was hired as a staffer?"

"Yes, we checked that of course, but the name and address were bogus, so was all her other information. No one there knew her. No one had ever seen her before. She was there for only one day, the new girl, but we have the rest of the staff working with a police artist to get a composite drawing of her. We're waiting for that now. I'm not too hopeful."

"Too many chefs in the kitchen?" Murdock asked.

"Yeah, something like that. You know, no one really saw her clearly or talked to her much. She worked off in a corner and did her work alone by herself, stuffing envelopes mostly, until she saw her chance."

"Damn!" Murdock growled. "Listen, Griff, you know a *Chronicle* reporter, Byron James?

"No, can't say as I do. Never heard of him. Why?"

Miles Murdock pulled out the "Murder Syndicate" clipping from that morning's *Chronicle* and handed it to the Homicide captain. Griffin read it and whistled.

"You know anything about that?" Murdock asked.

"No, no one here has suggested such a thing yet, but yes, these murders could be connected. They probably are, all done with a .38 and on some of them it seems the same woman was involved but... How does this reporter know so much? I mean, a murder for hire ring seems too much for me to swallow at this point in the investigation. We're just getting started here, Miles."

Murdock nodded, "While you and your men get started, Griff, I think the Purple Scar needs to get to work on this right away."

Captain Griffin nodded, "All right, but where will you look?"

"I'm going to find that reporter and speak to him first. Then I have a hunch about the widow Smith."

"Cathy Smith?"

"Yes," Murdock stated sharply.

"We already checked her out, my men talked to her at length. She says she doesn't know anything and we can't shake anything out of her but…"

"But what?" Murdock insisted.

"She's scared, Miles. Terrified of something or someone."

"Well her husband was murdered in cold blood, so maybe it's just that?" Murdock asked, but then shook his head slowly the more he thought it over.

"Yes, that's true, it could be that, but to me it seems that something else is scaring her," Griffith replied, "but she is shut as tight as a clam about it. She won't talk. Won't spill."

"That can be rectified," Murdock stated coldly. Then he got up from his seat, walked to the door of the Captain's office ready to leave.

"You'll keep me informed if you find anything, Miles?"

"Yes I will, and you do the same, Griff."

Captain Dan Griffin watched his friend leave his office. He liked Miles Murdock, had known him and his murdered brother John, for years. He did not exactly approve of Miles' activities as the Purple Scar but he realized that the masked man was certainly useful in some cases. None was more crucial than the one that had just been dropped into his lap now with the Carson murder. It was a political hot potato. It was one thing to have a few murders here and there in the city like the Alsace slaying or the Smith killing—those things happened every day or so in a big city like Akelton—but not the murder of a mayoral candidate. That kind of action needed to be answered by the police with results forthcoming very soon.

Captain Griffin sat back in his chair and thought about the Carson murder—an attractive successful reform-minded woman gunned down just before the election. She'd been ahead in the polls. Mayor Bradshaw wasn't a bad egg, but he was rumored to be corrupt. It certainly was very convenient for him that Carson now lay dead and out of the picture for the election. Still and all, Griffin had trouble accepting the thought that the mayor of all people might have been involved.

In a black sedan racing through the city to the Chronicle Building, those were the very same thoughts going through Miles Murdock's mind. Perhaps the mayor was involved? But if he was, how to get him to talk? Murdock knew it could prove impossible, something even the Purple Scar might not be able to accomplish.

Once at the Chronicle Building, Miles Murdock parked his sedan and went inside to see the reporter, Bryce James. Mr. James did not have a private office. Rather, the young man had a desk in "the swamp," the pool where stringers and newbie reporters worked out of. The area was loud and noisy with the ever-present clunking and pounding of typewriter keys and the swirl of cigarette and cigar smoke throwing a pall over the entire room. It looked like a swamp. It smelled like a swamp.

"You wanted to see me?" a young man looked up from his desk as Murdock came over and sat at the chair at the side of the man's desk.

"Yes, my name is…"

"I know; you're Doctor Miles Murdock. You're one of the highest-priced specialists in the city, but you also do a lot of pro-bono work for the poor at your clinic on Dawn Street."

Miles nodded, he was impressed. "You seem to know a lot, Mr. James."

"Bryce, please. I know some stuff. I'm not going to have my desk here in the swamp forever."

"I can see that," Murdock replied with a grin. "But I am here now because I need your help. I read your article about the Murder Syndicate and found it most interesting. I want to know where you came up with that idea?"

James smiled slyly, "Are you with the police, Doctor Murdock?"

"No, but I am assisting Captain Griffin of the Homicide Squad on this. You can call him if you like."

"No, that won't be necessary. So you want to know how I came up with the idea? I simply put the facts of the murders together then used a little creative license as would any good writer. I also spoke to Cathy Smith."

"Ah, now I see. So she told you… What?"

James laughed, "She told me nothing, Doctor Murdock. She was shut as tight as a steel drum. I couldn't get anything out of her."

"I see."

"No, you don't. Let me explain. We've had numerous murders in Akelton City in the last few weeks. Not all, but many seem to be the work of the same person or group of people. All were murdered with a .38 revolver, and in some of the cases a 'young woman' was described as leaving the scene. She was obviously the shooter. She was also obviously in disguise."

Murdock smiled, he was beginning to like this young reporter.

James nodded with a boyish grin, continued. "Anyway I back tracked on the murders, looking for clues and witnesses. Most of them have no connection with any other murders. I mean, take that lawyer Alsace, for instance."

"Yes, tell me about him," Murdock asked thoughtfully, wanting to examine what this young reporter might know.

"I am sure it was a hired murder, so the person who was his killer could have been anyone. I can not find a connection to anyone that makes sense. Neither can the cops. The same thing on the Carson murder…"

"Well, that may be, but there is one person who does benefit by one of these actions," Murdock stated sharply.

James looked over at the tall, trim and powerful man and into his piercing black eyes. "You're not saying the mayor ordered…?"

"It doesn't matter if he did or not, we'll never find out because he'll never talk," Murdock stated.

James nodded, "That's too bad."

"Too bad is not enough for us to solve these crimes, Mr. James. Tell me about what you found out from Cathy Smith."

"Not much, I'm afraid. Her husband had a girlfriend, the girlfriend is clean, knows nothing. The wife seems clean too but she's…terrified. She won't talk about it at all. I guess it's understandable under the circumstances but I get the feeling there is more to it than that. Like someone very terrible is scaring her."

"You are very perceptive. So what about this Murder Syndicate angle in your story?" Murdock insisted.

James just smiled, "A bit of melodrama, got me noticed, didn't it! All the murders seem connected somehow so why not consider some kind of Murder Syndicate? I know the name sounds like it came right out of one of those lurid pulp mystery magazines, but I intended it to read like that."

"I see," Murdock stated, a bit disappointed.

"Now what about you? A doctor investigating murders, isn't that a bit unusual and out of your normal line? Care to tell me why you are involved and what you plan to do?"

Miles Murdock smiled broadly, totally ignoring the younger man's question, "Mr. James, it has been a pleasure making your acquaintance and I foresee a brilliant career for you. If you can keep from getting yourself killed. Now I must be off."

+++

Murdock left James and the Chronicle Building and was back at his office on Swank Street within the hour.

"Tommy!" Murdock called out to his assistant and friend.

"Yeah, Boss, what's up?"

"You have some work to do tonight."

"Oh, boy! So the Purple Scar is going out on a mission?"

"Yes, but you are not going out with me. Instead I want you to take your slick second story abilities out of mothballs and post guard over a young *Chronicle* reporter named Bryce James. He's at work now at the Chronicle Building downtown. Put a tail on him when he leaves work, keep track of him if he goes out or home. His life may be in danger."

"He's the guy what wrote that Murder Syndicate article, ain't he, Boss?"

"Yes he is, Tommy."

"Then you better see this, it's the late city final of *The Chronicle*," Tommy said handing Murdock the newspaper. Across the top of the fold was splashed the headline, "'Murder Syndicate Terrorizes City'. In large print was the byline, 'Story by Bryan James.'

Murdock sighed deeply. "This is not good, Tommy. It may be good for James' career, just what he wants I'm sure, but it draws attention to him from the killers at a time when that might be the worst thing for him to do. Stay close on his tail and do everything you can to protect him."

"I will, Boss. Where are you going?"

"The Purple Scar has a visit to make to a very terrified woman."

Byron James saw the new edition of *The Chronicle* with the blasting headline about the Murder Syndicate story with his byline in large letters below it. It was the highpoint of the young reporter's career to date and he basked in the glory. James took one of the papers and proudly stashed it folded under his arm as he left the building. He'd mail the copy to his mother and father back in Iowa who had told him that becoming a newspaper reporter was dooming himself to utter failure. Tomorrow morning James had an appointment with Editor-in-Chief Sam Dragna who wanted him to take a bigger lead on more important stories. Dragna even intimated that since the office two doors down from his own was currently unoccupied; James might be slotted in there if he showed more of the kind of bold initiative he'd shown on the Murder Syndicate story.

Bryan James walked the dozen or so blocks to his apartment in a light-hearted gait. Things were finally working out well for him. Nevertheless he felt uneasy, for he noticed a man a ways back on the sidewalk who seemed to be following him. It might be nothing, and it probably was, perhaps just a product of his overactive imagination, but he began to grow concerned.

Still and all, earlier that day, that Doctor Murdock had complimented his work, however he'd also said he would have a good career if he didn't end up getting himself killed. James knew really good investigative reporters were often in danger. He walked faster. He heard the footsteps of the man behind him pick up their pace now as well. James grew nervous. He turned around abruptly, there was a young woman now walking right behind him. She was calm. Nicely dressed. Rather lovely. He boldly turned towards her.

"Excuse me, Miss, but can you help me, please?"

"Yes, what is it?" she asked seeming surprised by his attention and question but quite willing to help. That was good.

"See that man down the corner?"

She took a quick look down the block, "Yes?"

"I think he has been following me."

"Really? Why?"

"I... I don't really know, but I think I am in danger."

"Well, what do you want me to do?" she asked carefully, her eyes showing alarm but her lovely face most alluring.

"Well, do you think you could walk down to him, maybe ask him for directions to distract him, while I get away?" James asked. "I know it is asking a lot of a stranger but I'm really nervous about this."

"I don't know," the young woman said carefully, seeming a bit nervous herself now, weighing the request. "Look, why don't we just duck into this bar. I know the place and they have a back door that opens onto an alley on the next street. You can get away through there. What do you think?"

"Yes, that would work fine. Let's do it now. You lead the way and I shall follow," James was elated, and he was also quietly noticing the beauty of this slim young lady. She was quite the dish.

"I don't even know your name." James said as she lead him through the busy barroom towards the back of the building and then out the back door. She was right, it lead straight into an alley on the next street. James sighed with relief.

"My name is Dorothy," the young woman told him.

James smiled, "My name is Byron. Byron James."

"Yes, I know," she told him.

He looked at her with a smile. "You read my name in the paper?"

"Yes, I did," she said and smiled back at him. It was only then that he noticed the steel grey .38 she held leveled at him in her hand.

"You're...the killer?"

"And you're a very good reporter, Mr. James. Perhaps too good."

Then she pressed the trigger that ended a most promising career.

+++

It was night by the time Miles Murdock reached the Smith residence. Cathy Smith lived alone, now, a widow since the murder last week of her husband.

"So the woman is too terrified to talk?" Murdock whispered grimly as he took out the eerie rubber mask from his secret pocket and placed it over his head and face. He transformed himself into the Purple Scar and the visage of that terrible mask, now enhanced by the bizarre phosphorescent glow, was truly horrible to see. "She's too terrified to talk? Well, the Purple Scar will make her too terrified *not* to talk!"

The Purple Scar used his pencil flashlight to find the keyhole to the back door of the woman's house and took out his set of master keys and began working on the lock. In a matter of seconds he had the door open and was inside the dark house. He knew the woman lived alone and had no dogs or other animals. For that knowledge he was grateful as it would make his job tonight all the easier.

The man dressed as the Purple Scar slowly and quietly walked through the house, went up the stairs, and found the bedroom where Cathy Smith lay sleeping. He watched her for a moment as she slept so soundly, like she didn't have a care in the world. Well, not now! He looked at her carefully as he thought about her murdered husband. What did she really know? Something was wrong here. She was playing the victim but he did not believe she was a victim at all. He had a hunch that this woman all along had been behind her husband's murder and he was now determined to get to the truth.

The room was dark and quiet. Slowly the Purple Scar approached the bed where the sleeping woman lay. He was well aware his impending actions would terrify her, maybe even scare her to death, but he knew that is exactly what she needed to prompt her to talk. Murdock grabbed up the sleeping woman, shook her awake and then pressed the face of The Purple Scar in front of her own face so that the woman could see it plainly.

Cathy Smith screamed in terror but Murdock's hand quickly covered her mouth stifling her cry.

"I am here from the Murder Syndicate. Here to end your life if you do not answer all my questions truthfully. I am here to tie up loose ends from your contract on your husband's murder," the Purple Scar spoke in a hoarse whisper, a harsh tomb-like cadence. He allowed her wide eyes to get a good view of his purple glowing mask which really terrified her even more.

"You talked to the police!" The Purple Scar growled in anger.

"No! Never! I told them nothing!" she begged in abject terror. "I kept my part of the bargain, not to say one word. I swear it!"

The Purple Scar nodded, now he knew his hunch had been correct, she had been working with her husband's killers all along. Now all that was left was for him was to pry the specifics out of her.

"Talk now! Tell me all you know!" the terrifying purple face raged sheer menace.

"I can't, I promised," she pleaded. "You know, you told me about it; the Conspiracy of Silence."

"Explain it to me!" the man in the mask demanded.

Cathy Smith swallowed hard, "I never said a word to the police, or that reporter, I promise. When I found out that my husband was going to have me killed so he could take a new wife, I decided two could play at that game. I contacted you with a counter offer and you took it."

"I know all that!" the purple face whispered grimly. "What I want you to tell me about is your part in this Conspiracy of Silence."

"That's what you explained to me over the phone when I hired you," she stated, shaking now in fright. "You said how by my entering into a pact with you to have my husband killed, we were now partners in crime and I could never breathe a word of my knowledge of the murder without getting the electric chair myself. So I kept quiet. I could never talk. Like you told me, we were in a Conspiracy of Silence together."

"Good," the Purple Scar stated bluntly, but Murdock was shocked and alarmed by the depth of the crimes and their organization. "Now tell me, how did you find out about my organization and contact me?"

"I heard my husband on the phone one night…late… I wondered who he was talking to and why. I knew about his girlfriend, that tramp! When he went away I came down and saw the phone number scribbled upon a note pad. So I called it."

"And you said what?"

"I spoke to a man. You were that man. I told you my name was Cathy Smith and my husband had just spoken to you. I wanted to know what about."

"So tell me what I told you?"

"Why are you asking me this? You already know."

The Purple Scar held her closer, forcing his glowing face of twisted death into her own. "I ask the questions here! Understand!"

"Yes," she muttered meekly, shaking with renewed fear. "Please do not kill me!"

"No! Never! I told them nothing!"

"I will kill you if I desire. That is entirely up to you and what you tell me. Now answer my questions! What did I tell you?"

"You asked me if I wanted to make a counter offer. I said I didn't understand," she said haltingly, fearful. "You explained to me that my husband had contracted with you to have me killed, but if I would double the payment, you would accept my counter offer and have him killed instead. Then I was instructed to call you again after the job was done; verification would appear in the next morning's newspaper and I would make my payment. You told me to have the money ready and never tell anyone about this. Then you told me we were in a Conspiracy of Silence for I was just as guilty as were you of the murder if I ever talked."

"That is correct," the Purple Scar whispered quietly, then he added, "Do you still have that piece of paper with that phone number?"

"Y-yes," Cathy Smith told him shaking in terror.

"Give it to me now!"

The Purple Scar left the Smith home. The woman had given him the paper with the phone number on it and he had tied her up in bed without hurting her. He had scared the hell out of her though. She was tied up tight but not too tight, not so tight that she wouldn't be able to get herself loose soon; once he was long gone.

Murdock quickly withdrew the Purple Scar mask from his face and folded it up into a thin mass of rubber he deftly put away into the secret pocket of his coat. Then he got into his sedan and headed back to Swank Street in Akelton City.

On the drive back Murdock went over the complexities of the case in his mind. He was rather ashamed of his harsh treatment of Cathy Smith, using the Purple Scar to scare her like that, but he knew he had to do it that way in order to get her to talk. In any case, she was not innocent in her husband's murder. She could have reported to the police what she had discovered; instead she decided to take her own form of revenge. In truth, the killer's 'Conspiracy of Silence' creed was accurate, for she was just as guilty of her husband's death as was the actual murderer.

Miles Murdock looked at the paper with the phone number written upon it. It was an Akelton City number. Probably belonging to an office downtown, maybe even on Swank Street itself. He wondered who could be behind such a violent scheme. The very fact of a murder for hire ring operating in his city had him enraged into action. He had to find out who they were! To put a stop to them!

Murdock floored the gas pedal on his sedan. It was already morning and the sun was coming up. He decided to swing by Dale Jordan's apartment on the way to his office. Something told him he would need Dale's help on this case, as well as the help of Tommy and Captain Griffin if he was to break up this so-called Murder Syndicate and bring these killers to justice.

When Murdock got to Dale's apartment she was already up and having breakfast and quickly let him in.

"Miles, dear! Are you all right?" She ran to him, hugging him to her tightly. He held her to him as well, missing the feel of her warm yearning flash against his own. Dale was dearly in love with Miles, and he with her. Their long romance had not yet culminated in marriage and the family they both wanted, but for the time being Murdock's mission was his war against crime and that took precedence over all other concerns. Dale Jordan understood that and would do anything she could to help him in his mission.

"I was so worried about you, Miles," Dale cried, kissing his lips feverishly.

"I'm safe. I had a job last evening."

"I know. I spoke to Tommy," she said. "Listen, Tommy is really sorry, he feels terrible..."

Murdock broke away from Dale, looked at her carefully, "What do you mean, sorry? What happened?"

"It wasn't his fault, Miles. That reporter, Mr. James, he made Tommy, got spooked and then slipped away from him. James was found dead in an alley late last night. It's in the papers this morning," she handed Murdock that morning's edition of *The Chronicle*. "I'm sorry. And Tommy just feels terrible about it."

Miles Murdock sighed deeply. "I liked that kid, and he had real potential as an ace reporter. I sent Tommy out to keep an eye on him."

"Tommy is broken up about it, Miles."

"I know, he didn't expect to get made, and he didn't expect James to try to get away from him," Murdock read the article on the front page of *The Chronicle* that included a photo of a smiling Byron James. "It says here the police say an unknown young woman lead James through the bar and out the back door into an alley. That's where he was shot."

"That 'young woman' again, Miles?"

"Yes, we have a murder for hire ring operating in our city, Dale. The ring is run by a man, or so it appears, but it seems the assassin, or one of the assassins at least, is a rather lovely young woman. At least she's been described that way."

Dale Jordan shook her head in anger. "A pretty woman can get to a lot of people who would never suspect her, until it was too late, Miles. This woman is a cold-hearted killer. She's responsible for all these murders and the murder of Adele Carson as well. That was horrible. What's this city coming to?"

"We'll get her, Dale, and anyone else who is in league with her. Are you ready to go?"

"Yes."

"I have the black sedan parked downstairs, we'll run over to the office, collect Tommy, and then I have to make an important phone call."

"Boss, I don't know what to say," Tommy Pedlar said in an emotional outburst, for he had failed his friend and allowed a good man to be killed while under his watch. He had let down Mr. James and Murdock. "I'm so sorry; I feel all broke up about it."

"I know, Tommy, but you did what you could. Let's not mention it again."

"But it was that gal, Boss. I was following James a block behind him, not too close to spook him I thought, when all of a sudden I spot this gal walking right behind him. It was like she came out of nowhere. I increased my pace to catch up but then James noticed me and panicked. I saw them talk quickly, then she lead him into a bar. By the time I get there, James is dead and she's long gone."

"Did you get a description of her?" Murdock asked.

Tommy shook his head, "No, it was dark on the street and I was a ways behind them. I never saw her with him in the bar."

Miles Murdock nodded as Dale Jordan went over to console Tommy; the devastated second-story man known as the Sticky-fingers Kid, was distraught at his failure.

The three friends were quiet for a long moment and then the door to the office swung open and Captain Dan Griffin of the Homicide Squad came into the room.

"Griff, glad you're here. Now we can begin," Murdock stated.

"You got a phone number from the Smith woman?" Griffin asked eagerly.

"Yes," Murdock withdrew the small sheet of paper with a phone number scribbled upon it. "I only hope the number still works."

"What are you going to say?" Dale asked Murdock.

"I'm not quite sure. I'll play it by ear, see what I can learn, but I am going to try to hire him to have someone killed."

"Who you gonna have killed, Boss?" Tommy asked nervously.

"Yes, Murdock, I'd like to know that information in advance before you say a word to these people," Captain Griffin insisted.

"Who is it to be, Miles?" Dale asked haltingly.

"The Purple Scar," Murdock stated simply.

Dale, Tommy and Captain Dan Griffin each looked longingly at Miles Murdock.

"That's taking a big chance," Griffin told his friend.

"It has to be the Scar. I can't put anyone else in such jeopardy," Murdock said and the others slowly nodded in agreement.

"It's the smart play, Boss. I guess it is," Tommy said carefully, "but how are they going to find the Purple Scar to carry out the murder?"

"I'm going to tell them," Murdock said simply.

"Oh, Miles! That's too dangerous!" Dale cried.

"I have to agree," Griffin added. "Not a good idea."

"No, I have to do it that way, but I will do it right. We'll set a trap. I'll have Dale and Tommy with me and you'll have your men close by, Griff. We have to catch these people and put a stop to this Murder Syndicate once and for all. We have to do it for Adele Carson, for Bryce James, and for all the others they've killed."

Captain Griffin nodded, "All right, so where do we start?"

"I make the call," Murdock said simply.

"My people will trace it," the Homicide Captain added.

"I hope that number is still good, Boss," Tommy said dubiously.

"Well, we'll find out right now," then Miles Murdock picked up the telephone and had the operator put through a call to the number he gave her written on the paper he had taken from Cathy Smith.

"It's ringing," Murdock whispered softly.

Everyone waited with grim anticipation. The air in the room was supercharged with tension and electricity, as the phone rang once, twice, and finally a third time before the connection went through and someone at the other end picked up.

"Yes?" a cautious voice at the other end of the line answered in a terse one-word reply.

"I need a job done and was told to call this number for reliable service," Murdock said carefully.

"And who told you to call this number, bub?"

Murdock halted for a moment, thought fast, "Well, I'd rather not say. I don't like to talk about such things. You see, I was told about how important it is to keep a conspiracy of silence in these kinds of things. I believe that implicitly."

There was no answer from the man at the other end of the line, but he had not hung up either. Dale and Tommy looked closely at Miles, he was tense. Captain Griffin held up his hand with his finger to his lips to indicate silence.

Murdock took a deep breath, it was obvious the leader of the Murder Syndicate was thinking it over, but would he take the bait?

Then the mystery man at the other end of the line said, "I…think not. I am going to terminate this conversation. I am going to hang up now."

Murdock's hopes were dashed, he knew he had to say something fast to change the situation.

"No! Don't hang up! I need this job done and will pay triple your usual rate," Murdock pleaded, careful. "Money is no object."

The line went silent again.

Dale Jordan could feel her heart pounding in anticipation. Tommy Pedlar felt sweat trickle from his armpits down his sides. Captain Griffin looked over at Murdock and nodded meaningfully.

"All right then," the voice told Murdock. "Tell me the name of the person you want dealt with?"

Murdock swallowed nervously, "The Purple Scar."

There was more silence at the other end of the line.

Captain Griffin's mouth formed the silent words, "I think you've got him!"

Murdock shook his head, he wasn't so sure. He waited patiently for the voice to get back to him. He hoped the police trace would go through, the call had gone on long enough, but something told him the trace wouldn't work and that this was his only chance at these people.

The man got back on the line, "Your request is difficult and most unusual."

"I really must have this job done, please do not refuse me."

"I did not say we would refuse it."

Murdock nodded with a grim smile, appealing to the man's greed had been the right tack, "I can tell you precisely where he will be on a certain night and at a certain time."

"And who am I speaking with?" the man asked.

"Who am I speaking with?" Murdock countered.

"Conspiracy of Silence, remember that," the man told Murdock with dire menace in his voice. "Now, tell me where this Purple Scar can be found. You will see verification of the job in the next day's newspaper, then you will be contacted to make payment. I will give you a new number to call for the location for the payment."

"So you will do the job, then I pay you after it is done?" Murdock asked curiously, a bit surprised.

"Yes, you make payment when and how I tell you, or you will be the next victim," the man warned in a voice that promised utter doom.

Then the man gave Murdock a new phone number which he wrote down and he asked his final question.

Murdock looked at Griff and then nodded, "I have it on good information that the Purple Scar will break into the office of some rich guy on Swank Street, Doctor Miles Murdock. It will happen tomorrow night, at midnight."

Murdock gave the man the address.

Then the phone at the other end of the line went dead.

Murdock breathed deeply, letting out the nervousness he had allowed to bottle up within him, "We've done it! They'll be here tomorrow night!"

"And so will the Purple Scar and all the rest of us, Boss," Tommy spoke up.

Miles Murdock nodded grimly, put the two papers with the old and new phone numbers in his pocket, kissed Dale, and then asked Captain Griffin if anything had gone through on the trace of the phone call.

Griffin made a quick call to police headquarters, but when he got the news a gloomy look overtook his features. "It didn't go through, Miles. They tell me the killers used a separate line run from a phone booth. My men are at the phone booth now, but they say the call wasn't made from there. They found another line from that booth running into the Hermitage Arms Building across the street. They'd have to dig up the wire and run a physical trace to the particular apartment in that building. It's huge. It has over three hundred apartments. It would take all night and day to find it, and alert your killers. I told them to lay off for now, no use stirring up things and letting the killers know we're onto them."

Murdock nodded; it was as he had feared. "All that means is that it is up to The Purple Scar tomorrow night to capture the members of this Murder Syndicate."

Meanwhile, in a luxury Swank Street apartment ten blocks from where the lawyer Alsace had been murdered weeks ago and only two blocks from where Miles Murdock kept his office, two lovers were on a couch in a heated embrace.

"I love you, Charlie," the young woman who had gone by the name of Dorothy Vane told the young man as her lips brushed against his own in heated kisses.

"And I you, my dear," he spoke passionately as his lips covered her own. Their love making was wild and frenzied.

As the woman's heated kisses grew to a resounding crescendo, her hand most carefully and delicately reached for the steel grey .38 revolver that was in her purse and withdrew it. With cold professional precision and guile she raised the weapon so that the gun barrel was one inch from the temple of the unsuspecting young man. The young woman smiled grimly. She had him now!

"Ah, my love," the young man named Charlie muttered, "you are so lovely, so delicious to be with…"

"Charlie?" the young woman who called herself Dorothy Vane said with a smile as she drew her lips away from his, "I think I have you this time."

Charlie smiled triumphantly, "I think not, my love. For if you look down at the nape of your lovely neck, you will discover my sharp and shiny blade barely one-quarter of an inch from your lovely throat. I always told you a blade is far better than a gun for close work."

Dorothy nodded, laughing gaily, the game was over, she withdrew her .38 from the man's head and placed it back in her purse, as Charlie lowered his blade from her throat and deftly placed it in the sheaf on his belt.

"My darling, you are good, but not quite that good," Charlie told her with another kiss.

"Yes, but I'm getting better, Charlie," she told him, looking longingly into his coal-black eyes. Dorothy smiled then, for Charlie's eyes were just as dark as her own. "I am good enough to do most of our jobs here in Akelton City."

"Yes," Charlie admitted, "but soon we will move on as we always do. Not a good idea to stay in any one place too long. Ten—twelve jobs is the limit, then the police start to get ideas. By leaving after a few jobs and going to another city we get the jump on them and they can never connect the dots and find us. And by having you do most of the jobs here—well, no one would suspect a lovely young woman like you. It puts them all off their game."

Dorothy smiled, "And I enjoy doing it, Charlie. You should see the surprised looks on their faces when I plug 'em."

"...a blade is far better...for close work."

He laughed coldly, "I know."

She shrugged, "I do feel bad about that Carson woman, she was a nice lady and a decent person for a politician, but a job is a job."

"That's right and the money was big. However, I fear we may have made an error in taking the mayor's offer on that one. It brought down too much heat. I think this job tomorrow night will be our last one here in Akelton City. Then we'll blow town. Maybe winter down in Mexico or visit Europe for a vacation? We have more than enough dough. Then maybe we'll come back to the states in six months or so and do a few jobs in New York or Chicago. There's always a need for our kind of work in those cities."

"Okay, Charlie, that sounds grand. Maybe we can fit in a trip to Paris?"

"Sure thing, doll, but first we got that Purple Scar job," Charlie said thoughtfully, thinking it through.

"You look worried about it."

"Nah, just a bit concerned. It came as a referral, but most of our jobs come in that way. But this Purple Scar is a dangerous crime fighter in this town, so it is no wonder someone wants him dead. Our employer will pay us triple our going rate, so money is no object to him. I like that. Still and all, this could be a trap, so that is why I'm going to be there with you. If he has set a trap, he'll be the one to get trapped, not you. You'll be safe, doll."

"Oh, Charlie, you're so gallant. Did I ever tell you how much I love you?"

"Every day, doll, but I never get tired of hearing it."

+++

The next night as midnight approached all was in readiness for the trap Miles Murdock and his crew were set to spring, using The Purple Scar as murder bait. Tommy Pedlar was on station in the outer office; the first line of defense. In the lab, Miles Murdock was now dressed in black and wearing his Purple Scar mask, ready to go to his upstairs apartment and await the break-in and attack. He was even anticipating it.

Across the street, waiting for Murdock's signal was Captain Dan Griffin and half a dozen of his Homicide dicks, set to come to his aid should they be needed.

Murdock had had the devil of a time convincing his girl, Dale Jordan, to go back to her place and wait for news. He didn't want her to be placed in peril by tonight's action. After a heated argument, Dale relented and left. Murdock already missed her but was relieved she would not be here to be placed in danger. For he knew he was playing a deadly game. Murdock knew nothing about these killers, nor how many of them there were. He was taking a big chance by setting himself up as murder bait in order to catch them and he knew that it could all blow up in his face.

The chimes of the clock on the First National Bank Building next door struck midnight and Miles Murdock was ready. The lights in the lab were off and the eerie Purple Scar mask was now upon his face emitting a dull sinister glow from the phosphorescent sheen within the pliant rubber. He looked grotesque and terrifying and counted on that image to throw off his attacker. He checked his .38 revolver once again. He knew there would surely be gun work tonight. Now he walked upstairs to take his place in the darkness behind the door to his second floor apartment, waiting.

Tommy Pedlar likewise now lay in ambush in the pitch dark outer office on the first floor of Murdock's Swank Street building. He sighed deeply as he heard the outer door lock being tampered with and suddenly the door opened and a dark sinister shape entered the office. Tommy had been a good second-story man back in the day but he had never carried a gun. Instead, he knew how to use a blackjack quite well and he watched the intruder enter and move about the room as he got set to use his weapon. Tommy smiled now, it was the killer all right, and it looked to be a woman too. That caused him some concern about using the blackjack. Tommy followed the dark shape as she moved towards the stairways that lead to the second floor. He was right behind her and was thinking to disarm her when he suddenly felt a blow to the back of his head erupt like a volcano and he melted down into darkness.

"Charlie?" the woman by the stairs whispered softly in the dark.

"Sure, doll, I figured someone might be on guard here, so I got the drop on him while he followed you. I didn't want to shoot him and alert your victim. This one will be out for hours the way I slugged him. I'll hide this guy somewhere, now you go and complete the job."

Dorothy nodded, continued making a beeline in the dark office over to the stairway that lead to the private apartment of Miles Murdock on the second floor. This was the location she had been told where she would find the Purple Scar. The doctor who lived here was said to be out of town, but obviously this Purple Scar was seeking something in his private apartment upstairs, and he had men of his own stationed here. Dorothy was glad to have Charlie with her on this job tonight.

The building was quiet but there seemed to be mysterious movement within it. In the second floor apartment of Doctor Miles Murdock, the

Purple Scar stood waiting in the darkness with a cold .38 in his hand. He heard the light footsteps upon the stairs coming closer. It had to be the killer, and they were light footsteps so it had to be a woman, probably the same woman who had murdered all those others.

The door opened slowly, a sliver of light from the moon outside shone through the hallway skylight and offered scant illumination as the female form entered the private apartment. Dorothy didn't like the looks of this job now as it smelled like a trap, and the guard Charlie had conked on the head downstairs seemed to verify that feeling, but she trusted Charlie and his talent to ensure her success as he always had.

Dorothy entered the darkened room, gun in hand, looking for her victim the Purple Scar. She silently closed the door behind her when suddenly out of the dark a vicious blow hit her hand causing her to drop her weapon to the floor. She gasped, looking up at the dark shadow standing in front of her. It was a terrifying image. Her eyes grew wide with fear as she stared at the eerie purple glowing face that was now so close to her own. She was about to scream, scramble for her weapon on the ground, but the man held her fast. Then he suddenly flung her to the sofa across the room. The lights went on and Dorothy gasped in sheer terror at the face of her captor. For the image that confronted her was a man in black with a .38 leveled at her, but it was the face of that man that truly terrified Dorothy beyond anything she had ever seen in her life.

"The Purple Scar!" she shuddered, seeing the grotesque visage fully now that the lights were on. That face looked so much like a living corpse, a face with a bizarre phosphorescent sheen of red and purple burning flesh that looked like it had sprung from the very depths of hell itself.

"Yes, it is I," Murdock spoke from behind the mask in a harsh hoarse whisper. "You are the young woman who murdered the reporter Bryce James, reform candidate Adele Carson, and now has come here to murder me."

"No, I-I mean…" Dorothy Vane stammered. She did not know what to say to this terrifying monster. She could not look into the face of the man in front of her. It was just so hideous, so scary. It was not human! Now that the lights were on in the room and she could see it clearly and up close, the face seemed to be absorbing the light and radiating it back with a death-like glow from beyond the grave. And the scars on that face were ghastly, deeply etched masses of mottled and damaged skin. "No! Do not hurt me. I will tell you anything you want to know!"

"Yes you will, for there is no escape for you now," the Purple Scar told her. "Now how many of you are in this so-called Murder Syndicate?"

Dorothy stammered, "Just two, only Charlie and me."

Murdock nodded, so it was an independent operation after all. That was good because it would make them that much easier to put out of business, but that was also the reason they had been able to get away with their crimes. Murdock wondered where this Charlie was. He was about to give Captain Griffin the signal to bring in his men when the lights in the room suddenly went off, covering everything in darkness.

Murdock cursed himself for keeping all his attention on the woman and turning his back on the door and the light switch. He knew now that someone else had entered the room and it was not Tommy. Where was Tommy?

This newcomer into the now pitch dark room had to be a confederate of the killer, the man she had called Charlie. So now there were two killers loose!

Murdock realized he was in trouble now because they could see him in the dark! The same phosphorescent mask that had instilled such terror into the woman now made it possible for her and her intruder companion to see him. They could not see him clearly, but they could just make out his face in the darkness. Murdock swirled, thought he saw the outline of someone behind him, then felt a sharp blow to the head. He went down dropping his .38 to the floor in the pitch black room.

Murdock was stunned but not out. He scrambled on the floor seeking his weapon even as he was set upon by his attacker. This time it was a man. So the woman did have a male companion. Murdock fought the man in a fierce hand to hand battle upon the floor of his apartment in the utter blackness of the room. The fight was fast and furious with brutal punches being reined by and upon both men.

"I found my gun, Charlie," a woman's anxious voice suddenly blurted, "but I'm afraid to shoot him in the dark with you both fighting so close together."

"Get the lights!" the intruder's voice responded between sharp gasps of breath.

The two men continued their fierce fight in the darkness. The Purple Scar desperately trying to take the gun away from his attacker, while his attacker attempted to point his weapon at the crime fighter and fire. Suddenly the lights in the room went on again, followed a second later by multiple gun shots. However, these shots were not from the gun that the Purple Scar and his attacker were fighting to control.

Both men looked up and over at the tableau that was unfolding before them by the door. They could plainly see two figures there now that the lights were on again.

"Dorothy!" The man named Charlie shouted.

"Dale, what are you doing here?" The Purple Scar blurted in shock, realizing in an instant all that had happened.

Dale Jordan had defied Miles Murdock's wishes and returned to his office. She found that Tommy was missing from his post downstairs and suspected the worst. Then she entered the second floor apartment and turned on the lights to see The Purple Scar and his attacker battling for their lives for the attacker's gun. Dale instantly saw Dorothy now holding her own .38 seeking to fire the weapon in the melee between Charlie and the Purple Scar.

Both woman's eyes locked upon each other and they fired. Guns went off. Slugs entered soft female flesh. Both women were hit. Dale Jordan fell back against the door, a bloody wound to her left shoulder, while Dorothy Vane fell to the floor. Two slugs in her chest.

"Dale!" Murdock cried out in fear, still fighting off his attacker.

"Dorothy!" Charlie shouted in desperation, battling the masked avenger.

Then the Purple Scar saw his chance and grabbed his attacker's gun away from the man and quickly bashed him in the head with the cold metal of the weapon's barrel. Charlie slumped to the floor stunned as the Purple Scar jumped up and ran towards Dale.

"You've been shot!" Murdock cried as he took Dale in his arms.

"I'll live. I'm fine, just a scratch, but that woman on the floor needs a doctor right away," Dale replied softly.

"You never listen to me," Murdock chided as he examined Dale's wound.

"Good thing too," she replied with a grin, kissing the Purple Scar, as he checked to see that her wound was not serious. He kissed her again hard and long.

Dale said, "I love you, Miles. And Guess what? I found Tommy, and he's okay. He had a bad knock to the head by your friend there. He'll be fine, but he'll have a mighty bad headache for a while."

"Good, I was worried about him when he didn't show up as we planned," Murdock told her. He quickly made an improvised tourniquet for Dale's upper arm that stopped the bleeding. The bullet had gone right through the fleshy part of her shoulder. It was a clean wound and not serious.

"I'll be all right. See to that woman now. She's in a bad way." Dale told him.

The Purple Scar nodded, he could already hear Captain Griffin and his men entering the building and charging up the stairs, as he examined the two wounds in the woman named Dorothy. She was in a bad way, but he stopped the bleeding as best he could to stabilize her. There was not much he could do for her here, even with his laboratory downstairs, for this woman needed to get to City Hospital right away and get into an operating room with emergency surgeons.

"Dale, call for an ambulance," Murdock said. "I'm going to tie up this Charlie character into a nice bundle for Captain Griffin."

At that very moment Captain Dan Griffin and his men of the Homicide Squad burst into the room and he ordered his men to take Charlie into police custody.

"You did it!" Captain Griffin shouted in delight, looking towards the Purple Scar, unable to stop an involuntary shiver at the sight of that ghastly face.

"The Purple Scar did it, Captain," Murdock replied, then pointed towards Dorothy, "This woman needs an ambulance and has to get to City Hospital right away."

"We're on it; we have an ambulance outside waiting. I figured there'd be gunplay tonight," the Captain looked at the two women, then shrugged, "just never figured it would be between Dale and that murderous vixen over there."

"Murderous vixen is a good name for her," the Purple Scar stated coldly. "She is a dangerous psychopath, a shame the doctors will have to work so hard to save her life just so she and her companion, Charlie here, can go to the electric chair for all the killings they've done. The case of the Murder Syndicate is now closed. Almost. I have just one more item left to do."

"Almost?" Griffin asked surprised.

"Almost," The Purple Scar continued sharply. Then the masked man spoke two words into Charlie's ear that caused the killer's eyes to bug in total fear. He said, "Adele Carson."

"I can't talk about that," Charlie whispered nervously.

"It's the only way you might save Dorothy from the chair," the Scar added bluntly.

Charlie shivered and nodded, now defeated, "Okay, I'll spill."

"Then tell me now, right here, all of it," The Purple Scar demanded, and Charlie quickly whispered his words into the ear of the masked avenger.

Captain Griffin and his men then put Charlie in handcuffs and escorted him out of the room. On his way out the door the killer looked back at the face of the Purple Scar, winced with dread and said, "You're one ugly bastard! You know that? Now that I see you in the full light I understand why so many people are scared of you!"

"You are looking at the face of a corpse!" The Purple Scar said plainly in a hoarse tomb-like whisper. What Murdock wore upon his face was the death mask of his murdered brother, John, but he wore it proudly. He added in a grim voice, "Death waits for us all."

✝✝✝

The room was cold. Really cold. The luxury apartment on the Thirtieth Floor of the Halls Towers had the bedroom window wide open letting in the autumn coldness and wind. At that altitude the room was downright frigid and the man sleeping in the bed was feeling that coldness.

He woke up! Startled, freezing, shivering.

"Why is it so damn cold in here!" he blurted through chattering teeth, groggy with sleep but the chill was shocking him awake. "Who the hell left the window open?"

The man got out of bed, walked over to the wide, large window. The big glass window was fully raised, so was the screen. That was very unusual.

"Good evening, Mayor Bradshaw," a hoarse voice croaked out of the stygian darkness from across the room.

"Who is it? Who is there?" Bradshaw cried out, frozen with fear and cold now.

"The Purple Scar," Murdock stated in a defiant growl. "Look over here and you will see my face in the night."

"Arghhh! Oh my God!"

"Pretty, is it not?" a harsh sardonic voice growled.

Mayor Bradshaw gasped in terror. He could just make out eerie red and purple scars set in a terrible face that looked like it came from the very grave itself. He froze in fear staring at that horrible face.

"What do you want?" the mayor stammered.

"You. I want you. I want you to pay for your crime."

"What crime?" Bradshaw cried, stalling for time, thinking desperately.

"Adele Carson, Mr. Mayor. I know all about it," the Purple Scar said simply. The killers have told me all. They will tell the police everything first thing tomorrow morning and then the police will come for you. They will hunt you down if you run. The newspapers will report it all, the scandal will be huge, the courts will rule against you. And finally, you will get the electric chair. All for Adele Carson, Mr. Mayor."

"No!"

"Yes! You have no choice now."

"What of my wife? My poor children? I love them dearly."

"Yes, what of them, Mr. Mayor?" The Purple Scar asked sharply.

"It would destroy them!"

"Then I think it best you take matters in hand here and now before the killers speak of your part in this to the police," the Purple Scar demanded, now pointing a long bony finger towards the open window. "You can not change what you have done, but you can minimize the damage to your wife and family. If you care to do so."

"I see," Bradshaw muttered, shaking in fear as he starred at the wide open window. "Yes, I see."

"It is your one way out," the Scar told him simply.

"My one saving grace?" Bradshaw asked in utter defeat.

"Exactly," the Scar answered.

"Then I shall take it!" the mayor shouted coming to decisive action, suddenly running towards the open window and leaping out of it.

There was stark quiet in the room for a long moment, with only the screams of the mayor heard on his way down to the ground below.

The Purple Scar nodded with satisfaction, justice had been served. Then he left the room and headed back to Dale and Tommy.

Dale Jordan sat down on the couch uttering a tired sigh as she looked over at Miles Murdock, "Well, it was a wild night. Are you all right?"

"I'm fine now, but I'm still upset you came back here and took that bullet," he chided her with gentle anger. Now that they were alone and Murdock had returned from his mission with the mayor, he had taken off the Scar mask and placed it into the secret pocket of his jacket. Now that the case was closed he'd return the mask to the safe in his lab downstairs later. Until it was needed again. Right now all he wanted was to spend some time with Dale Jordan.

"Well, I'm glad I came back to check up on you, Miles. It turns out you needed me."

"You're right, I did need you and thank you," Miles said sitting down close to her on the couch.

"You know I love you, Miles," Dale told him, looking into his dark eyes, looking at his own handsome face now, which was so different from the grotesque death mask he wore of his brother when playing the part of the Purple Scar.

"And I you, Dale," Murdock replied returning a longing look into her eyes.

Just then the door burst open and Tommy Pedlar ran into the room. "Boss, you okay? Dale, my God, you're wounded! W-what happened?"

"What happened to you?" Murdock countered with a smile, glad to see his friend alive and apparently all in one piece.

"Ah, that bum got the drop on me, slugged me from behind, he did. I never saw it coming. I've got the headache to end all headaches, but I'm okay. So how did it all turn out, Boss?"

"We'll tell you all about it a bit later, Tommy," Murdock told him with a wink. "Now, why don't you find something to do and allow me and Dale some time alone."

Tommy smiled broadly, "Oh sure, I get it, Boss. I'll just be on my way, not bothering either of you two any more, but just answer me one question first before I leave."

Dale Jordan and Miles Murdock looked up at the former second story man with curiosity and a hint of exasperation, waiting for his question.

"Well?' Murdock asked.

Tommy gave a boyish grin, asked simply, "Did we win, Boss?"

"Yes, Tommy, we won," Murdock replied with a hearty laugh.

When Tommy Pedlar left the room Miles Murdock took Dale Jordan in his arms and kissed her like she'd never been kissed before. It was a moment both of them wished would never end. A moment both of them wished would last forever.

THE END

PURPLE THOUGHTS

Miles Murdock, M.D., was a Renaissance Man of the 1930s pulps who fought crime in mythical Akelton City. He was a world renowned plastic surgeon and master psychologist but his mission was to avenge his murdered policeman brother, by fighting criminals; and he did that in a unique and bizarre way.

The discovery of his dead brother's body had been a turning point in Murdock's life and stoked him with a fierce determination and a sacred mission. What had been done to his brother's face had not only shocked Miles Murdock to the core of his being, it haunts him from that day on. Since that day, the young doctor vowed to fight crime and track down the man responsible for his brother's murder. Thus The Purple Scar was born and began hunting down criminals wearing a gruesome purple mask which filled all who saw it with terror, even as it hid Murdock's true identity from criminals and the police alike.

The Purple Scar, or just "The Scar" as he was sometimes called, wore a mask that was an exact replica of the horribly disfigured death mask of Murdock's murdered brother. That mask recreated all the vicious scars and damage Murdock had seen upon his dead brother's face and recreated them in the gruesome purple death hues caused by the acid the killer had thrown upon his brother, acid that had eaten away the once handsome face of Murdock's beloved sibling. It was a horrific image.

Accompanied by a small group of friends who know his secret identity and aid him in his efforts, Miles Murdock takes us on exciting adventures fighting criminals as the mysterious Purple Scar.

When Ron Fortier of Airship27 Productions asked me if I wanted to try my hand at a new Purple Scar story, I jumped at the chance. I was thrilled to include my take on these classic stories about this amazing masked hero and crime fighter in this new book of Purple Scar adventures. I see my story as homage to this pulp hero, and the hero pulps in general. My aim was to tell my tale just as the stories were written long ago, back in the classic days of the pulps, way back in the 1930s. It was great fun to write. I hope that joy comes through to you as you read the story.

In "The Murder Syndicate," we find that various unrelated people are being murdered by a mysterious killer, who appears to be a lovely young woman. The police are baffled. There seems no connection between any of the victims.

At the same time Miles Murdock has just completed a new experimental mask, one that includes phosphorescent colors that give it an even more eerie and fearful look. It glows in the dark and is truly horrific. This is my one original addition to the series and I think it works well. I am sure that a scientist such as Miles Murdock would constantly be experimenting with new and improved versions of his mask in order to better impart doom and fear into his adversaries. He uses that new mask now as he begins his mission to track down the killer or killers and bring them to justice.

By then, the vicious and cold-blooded killer stalking Akelton City has become bolder, going so far as to murder a newspaperman friend of Murdock, and even a mayoral candidate. Now the stakes are greater and the pressure to find the killers is paramount. The Purple Scar and his three helpers soon find themselves knee-deep in the case when Murdock devises a deadly trap to set himself up as the next target of these mysterious killers who have been dubbed by the press, The Murder Syndicate. The results are shocking and violent and are set in the best tradition of the hero pulps. I hope you enjoy this story and that you will want to see more adventures of this most unique crime-fighting pulp hero — The Purple Scar.

GARY LOVISI - is a writer, editor, book collector and publisher, not always in that order. He loves the classic pulp magazine heroes and the excitement of pulp writing. Aside from his story featuring The Purple Scar in this volume, he has written stories about other classic pulp heroes such as The Moon Man and The Crimson Mask for Airship27 publications, as well as The Phantom Detective forthcoming from Airship 27.

Lovisi's latest books include *Sherlock Holmes: The Baron's Revenge* (Airship27, tpb), in which The Great Detective fights one of the most vile villains he has ever faced in his distinguished career. This original novel is a sequel to one of the best Holmes stories written by Arthur Conan Doyle, "The Adventure of The Illustrious Client". *The Baron's Revenge* is an amazing adventure in the style and mood of the original Doyle stories and characters. Other books by Lovisi include, *The Moon Man* (Airship27), which contains two of his stories about this unlikely Robin Hood of the pulps.

More recent books by Lovisi include *Mars Needs Books* (Borgo/ Wildside Press, tpb) a science fiction novel that mixes aspects of Philip K. Dick and the novel *1984* with, of all things, paperback collectors on

Mars!; *Violence Is The Only Solution* (Borgo/Wildside Press Double, tpb), collects three ultra hard-boiled Vic Powers crime stories; *More Secret Adventures of Sherlock Holmes* (Ramble House Books, tpb & hc) is a sequel to his earlier bestselling Holmes collection (*Secret Adventures of Sherlock Homes*) and contains three excellent original Holmes stories. Lastly, there is the edited anthology *Battling Boxing Stories* (Borgo/Wildside Press, tpb) which collects 15 fantastic hard-hitting tales of the pugilistic arts by some of the best and hottest authors writing today.

Lovisi is also the publisher of Gryphon Books which publishes new and classic reprint pulp crime and science fiction books. He is the editor of *Paperback Parade*, the world's leading and longest running magazine on collectable paperbacks of all kinds, and *Hardboiled* magazine, the hardest little crime fiction magazine in the world. He is also the sponsor of an annual rare book show, *The New York Collectable Paperback & Pulp Fiction Expo*, now in its 25th year! You can find out more about Gary Lovisi, his books and various publications, or contact him via email at his website: www.gryphonbooks.com

ADDING HORROR

One of the joys of producing new pulp anthologies of old pulp heroes is the wide ranging education in pulps I've received through this endeavor. It has often been a revelation as to the originality and bizarreness of some of these creations. The original pulps were a heady smorgasbord of every imaginable shading one can imagine in producing unique heroes and none was weirder than the Purple Scar.

Miles Murdoch is the quintessential pulp hero; handsome, rugged, an ex-college athlete, and as the series opens, one of the country's leading plastic surgeons. His brother is a police officer brutally gunned down by mobsters. They then proceed to throw acid on the dead man's face before dumping his body into the river. When it washes ashore, the visage is so horribly scarred as to be a gruesome mask of horror. Upon seeing it, Miles' own sanity takes a drastic detour as his souls begs to deal out justice to the men who murdered his beloved brother.

Using his skills, he makes a pliable rubber mask of that horrible face, scars and all. *"I'll use the mask only when I want it known the Purple Scar is on the trail."* And so the Purple Scar is born. He was created by writer John S. Endicott for the pages of "Exciting Detective" from Better Publishing Inc.

What appealed to me, upon discovering this creepy avenger was indeed that element of horror infused into the concept. Oh sure, many other pulp heroes such as the Green Ghost and Mr. Death had their own macabre appearances they used to scare their enemies. But none of them was as frightening as an actual, purple death-mask and imagining a criminal coming upon it in a darkened room immediately conjures up a powerful, gut-wrenching reaction. Those others may have aspired to be scary but the Purple Scar really was.

Thus when putting forward the call to our writers, I made it quite clear we wanted to see stories that would emphasize that horror element. Sure there would be action and mystery as are present in all masked avenger tales of this ilk, but with the added spice of genuine terror. Writers Jim Beard, Jonathan Fisher, Gene Moyers and Gary Lovisi all answered that challenge brilliantly and delivered four truly fun stories.

Whereas artist Richard Serrao blew us away with his interpretation of the Purple Scar. It was as if he could see into the soul of the tortured Miles Murdoch. His interior illustrations are perfectly suited to these tales and his cover, brilliantly colored by Shannon Hall, is a stark, dramatic experience we know our fans are going to relish.

So there you have Airship 27 Productions' first Purple Scar anthology. Several years in the making, we think it was worth the wait and that you'll agree. If you want to see more of this macabre death-dealer of justice, drop us a line and let us know. Till then, as ever, thanks for your continued support.

Ron Fortier
10/4/2014
Fort Collins, CO
(www.airship27.com)
(airship27@comcast.net)

Airship
27

Concept Drawings

GEORGE CHANCE
THE
GREEN GHOST

Volume One

Former stage magician George Chance, by various twists of fate, becomes an eerie vigilante to help the police solve baffling, unique mysteries. He is aided by his loyal crew made up of former glamour girl, Merry White, circus little man, Tiny Tim Terry, former bookmaker and gambler Joe Harper and Glenn Saunders, a novice magician who is his identical double. Created by writer G.T. Fleming-Roberts, the Green Ghost and his team battled all manner of villainy in some of the most macabre pulp adventures ever recorded.

Chance & Company are back in four brand new tales as chronicled by a quartet of today's finest New Pulp writers; Michael Panush, Greg Hatcher, B.C. Bell and Erwin K. Roberts. In these pages the Green Ghost will face a giant mechanical monster on a long abandoned boardwalk, attempt to solve the murder of his old mentor and uncover a ring of foreign saboteurs using radio frequencies to carry out their missions of terror and destruction. Pulp thrills and spills showcase one of the most original classic pulp heroes ever invented. Brought to you by Airship 27 Productions, the new home of High Adventure.

AN AIRSHIP 27 PRODUCTION

AIRSHIP27HANGAR.COM

NEW **PULP**

PULP FICTION FOR A NEW GENERATION!

CHECK AVAILABILITY AT: AIRSHIP27HANGAR.COM

A Son's Revenge

Veteran Police Sergeant Clarke is gunned down by hoodlums, shot in the back of the head. As he lay dying, a rush of blood to his face formed a macabre mask, a crimson mask! When his son, Doctor Robert "Bob" Clarke, saw that strange stigmata he interpreted it as a sign, inspiring him to become his father's avenger, the Crimson Mask!

Once again Airship 27 Productions digs into the dusty vaults of long forgotten, second tier pulp heroes to revitalize another great character in brand new, exciting adventures. Writers J. Walt Layne, Terrence McCauley, C. William Russette and Gary Lovisi took on the challenge of creating new, bizarre mysteries for the pharmacist turned crime-fighter and in doing so have put together a terrific collection of fast paced pulp action echoing the thrills of the original classics.

Aided by retired Police Commissioner Warrick, his former college roommate David Small and lovely nurse Sandra Gray, the Crimson Mask must hunt down the villainous distributors of tainted heroin, stop an invisible thief, learn who ignited the latest city gang war and solve the mystery of a killer targeting his father's allies.

Hold on to your fedoras, jump on the running board and get ready for blazing thrills galore, pulp fans, as the Crimson Mask is back!

AIRSHIP27HANGAR.COM

NEW PULP

PULP FICTION FOR A NEW GENERATION!

CHECK AVAILABILITY AT: AIRSHIP27HANGAR.COM

DEATH BENEATH THE WAVES

When several cargo ships begin disappearing on the waters of the Aegean Sea rumors begin to spread about black-armored demons rising up out of the deep. For Challenger Storm and his MARDL team, these events hold no particular interest until one of Storm's troubleshooters, Diana St.Clair, informs him that her former lover, and one-time MARDL scientist, Herbert Chambers is among the missing.

Later, a freakish wave wipes out a small Greek fishing village leaving only a handful of survivors. Is it possible someone has learned how to control the seas to do their bidding? When Storm and his companions arrive at a mid-ocean refueling station, they are attacked by saboteurs wielding bizarre rifles that fire sea-water.

Who is the mysterious figure calling himself Poseidon and what is the secret of his ability to create monstrous tidal waves? Can Challenger Storm find his underwater base in time to stop this mad genius before he rains down more watery destruction upon unsuspecting coastal populations? Is mankind doomed to be ruled by a new King of the Seas?

Here is high-octane pulp adventure on...and below the waves!

PULP FICTION FOR A NEW GENERATION!

FOR AVAILABILITY CHECK: AIRSHIP27HANGAR.COM

Made in the USA
Monee, IL
20 June 2020